Never Trust a Broken Heart

Ivy Symone

Acknowledgments:

I must acknowledge and give a major shout out to all of my readers! Without you guys, I wouldn't be so driven and motivated. I love being stalked for my follow up work. Love it! I appreciate all of the love and support you guys have shown.

Most importantly, I'd like to thank my mother Brenda Lockett, my cousin Geneva Mitchell, daughter India Bradford, and my sister Ebony Woods for being encouraging. Love you guys! Oh, and hey to my little ones Harrah, AJ, and Dion who have worked all of my nerves! Love you!

Contact Info:

Email: ivysymone@yahoo.com

Twitter: @ivysymone

Instagram: ivysymone

Facebook: Ivy Symone

Chapter 1

"Get yo ass up!"

Miki jumped out of bed, instantly awakened at the roar of his voice.

"Go to the mothafuckin' kitchen. Now!"

Rattled, it took Miki a minute to realize she was in trouble. She dared not ask what the problem was. Redd always wanted her to know what the problem was before he showed her. Miki wasn't a mind reader but she knew Redd like a book.

With Redd closely behind her, Miki stumbled her way to the untidy kitchen. Wiping her eyes she stood there nervously.

"Why the fuck this kitchen look like this?" Redd wanted to know.

"I fell asleep," was the only answer Miki could offer.

"You fell asleep?" he scoffed. "I bet yo ass was on that phone though."

Miki had been on the phone. She cooked dinner, fed the kids, and talked to her mother and her friend Kat. Time slipped away. She gave the kids baths and put them to bed. She fell asleep in Téa's bed after Téa insisted on her reading them, Téa and Chanta, a book. Miki awakened and trudged to her bedroom and got in bed.

"Clean up this goddamn kitchen," he barked. He added, "And fix me something to eat."

Miki looked at the time displayed on the microwave. It was almost three in the morning. She couldn't complain. She wouldn't. Miki wouldn't argue about his whereabouts either. She already knew the answer to that. It angered her though. He could be out all night long, laid up with another female, come home at whatever hour, and expected perfection from her. Miki was getting very tired of this life.

She fixed him a plate of what she cooked earlier. Then she busied herself in the kitchen.

After about fifteen minutes, Redd called her from the family room. "Miki!"

She immediately dropped what she was doing to tend to his need. "Yes?"

"What is this?" Redd asked holding up a small piece of paper.

Uneasiness settled over her. Miki knew what the piece of paper was. It was nothing really. Just some number a guy gave her earlier when she stopped at the gas station. She didn't dispose of it because when she was talking to Kat, her friend tried to convince her she should call him. Not thinking, Miki left it on the coffee table.

"I'm not gonna ask you again," Redd said with a threatening tone.

"It's just some number," Miki responded quietly.

"What the fuck did I--get over here!"

Miki was hesitant as fear built up in her. "Redd, I'm not gonna use it."

"I said get over here," he demanded again through clenched teeth.

"Redd, don't hit me," Miki pleaded taking small steps towards him.

"You a dumb ass hoe! When you gon' mothafuckin learn?"

Miki froze with fear as he leaped from the sofa. She knew she couldn't outrun him. He pounced on her delivering a blow to the left of her face. She cried out in pain.

"Let me catch you with another mothafuckin number! Where is your phone? Get me your damn phone! You think I'm playing Miki."

Miki wanted to run. She looked at the French doors leading to the outside deck. She tried to calculate in her head how fast she would have to be and how swift she would need to be to unlock the door, turn the knob and open it.

"Go get your phone! Now!"

Miki already knew there was incriminating evidence in her phone that could get her choked. Now she had to figure out how she could get rid of those things before handing over her phone. She could delete as she made her way back to the family room.

That plan crumbled when Redd decided to follow her upstairs to their master suite. He saw her phone on the nightstand and grabbed it. Knowing her unlock code Redd started going through the phone.

Miki glanced over at the adjoining master bathroom. That was her only hope. She eased a step over while still keeping her eyes on him

"Where you going? Whose number is this? You talked for forty minutes, then another hour..."

Miki looked at the number he was referring to. "That's Kat. She got a new number. Redd, I'm not talking to nobody."

"Shut up," he mumbled. "Why the fuck Kendrick number

staying in your phone? Didn't I tell you to stop talking to his bitch ass!"

"He just called to see how I'm doing," Miki explained.

"I'ma have to pay that nigga a visit," Redd said. "He don't need to fucking worry 'bout how my woman doing."

Miki exhaled heavily. *Please don't go to the text messages*, she thought. That was Redd's next move. He frowned, then looked at the phone with doubt, then frowned again. In an instant he punched Miki again, this time it sent her stumbling back.

"So, you wanna leave me!"

Miki cowered, pleading and crying, "No, I don't. I just want you to treat me better Redd."

"Bitch, I oughta knock all your goddamn teeth out," he spat venomously. "You telling that nigga you wanna leave me!"

He looked at the phone again. "And he asking you for pussy too? So, you fucking him Miki?"

"No!" Miki cried backing away from him. "I'm not. Please Redd. Don't!"

Redd started removing his belt. "Take your clothes off," he ordered.

Miki looked up into his eyes and they appeared red like he had turned into the devil himself. "Baby please! I don't want him...I told him that."

"Take your clothes off," he repeated, this time through clenched teeth. His eyes appeared as if they were flames.

"Please..." Miki sobbed.

The belt struck her on the left. It whipped around to her

back where it stung the most.

"If I gotta whoop your ass every mothafuckin day before you realize I ain't playing with you, then that's what the fuck I'ma do...Now, remove your shit."

The doorbell rang furiously waking Bebe from a deep sleep.

Who the fuck was that, he wondered.

His bedroom door was pushed open. Appearing at his bedside was a little girl with an unruly head full of hair and a big black Rottweiler/Doberman mix. Kennedi said in her soft voice, "Daddy, there somebody at the door."

Bebe got up out of bed. He was still sleepy and whoever this was at his door was about to get cussed out. Upon passing his living room he saw there was a box of cereal on the coffee table, colored balls of cereal on the floor, milk puddles everywhere, and an open jar of peanut butter.

Shadow stared back at him licking his chops.

"Kennedi, what is this?" Bebe asked trying not to show his anger.

Kennedi didn't hesitate when she replied, "Shadow did it."

"He's a damn dog," Bebe said. "And what's the purpose of the peanut butter?" The doorbell rang again this time with pounding. He could hear the familiar female's voice coming from the other side of the door.

"C'mon! Open up the damn door!"

Bebe went to the door and swung it open. Through gritted teeth he said, "Stop ringing my goddamn doorbell!"

"It took you long enough," Stefani sneered stepping aside so BJ could walk in. "Take him to school. I'ma be late for work." She bent down to kiss the top of BJ's head. "Bye baby. Mama'll see you later."

Kennedi called from behind Bebe, "Bye Stefani!"

Stefani crooned, "Bye babygirl." She looked at Bebe with a smirk, "Bye sweetie."

Bebe rolled his eyes and shut the door on her.

"Aw," BJ giggled at the mess Kennedi and her partner Shadow made. "Daddy, you see what they did?"

Kennedi said, "Nuh-uh. My not do it. Shadow did."

"BJ, help your sister get that up. I oughta whoop your ass Kennedi," Bebe said as he made his way back to his bedroom.

The good thing about working for himself was he could be as late as he needed to be. Between Stefani and some other family member he was guaranteed to run behind just about every morning.

Stefani was working his nerves though. Every time he turned around she needed something. She wouldn't let him have BJ yet Bebe was doing most of the parenting. He didn't want his son out of spite or to be malicious. Bebe knew he was in a better position to care for BJ than Stefani. She was unstable and still young minded. No matter how much money Bebe gave her, Stefani always came up short. Furthermore, she had men in her life but they only wanted one thing out of her. Bebe didn't blame them because that's how she carried herself. Hell, he fell for it too. Now they shared a six-year-old son.

Kennedi lived with him and he had full custody of her. Her mother, Sharonda, lost primary care of her when the state took

Kennedi and her siblings away because of child neglect, abuse, and abandonment. One of Sharonda's other baby daddies contacted Bebe to come to Sharonda's house one day. Terrell said he went to Sharonda's place to check on his two kids by her because they had called him wanting him to pick them up.

When Terrell got there, he discovered four of her kids including Kennedi, all under the age of eight by themselves, dirty, hungry, and scared. There was no food left for them to eat. The oldest left in the house had cut herself badly trying to open a can of soup for them. The house was a mess and filthy. The oldest of Sharonda's children who was twelve had left.

Bebe wanted to kick Sharonda's ass so bad. She was too old to still be living like that. She was thirty-three and was always putting a man first. Sharonda went out of town with her man leaving the twelve-year-old in charge. She had been gone a week.

Bebe scoffed at himself. His two baby mamas. Of all women to have his kids he picked two of the worst ones. Well Sharonda picked him. She said her tubes were tied. Stefani...he was completely irresponsible. For a moment he thought he could change her and actually have a real relationship with her. It didn't work.

After getting himself ready for work, he got Kennedi prepared for school. He fussed at her, "Kennedi, you know they feed you breakfast at school. You ain't gonna eat theirs if you eating Berry Crunch here."

"Daddy! Shadow did that. Shadow was hungry."

Bebe looked at Shadow. The dog looked back at him like: C'mon man, you know I ain't done shit. Bebe chuckled, "So that's what you sticking with babygirl?"

“Shadow did it,” Kennedi insisted.

Before leaving Bebe made sure to set Shadow out his food and water. Since Bebe made Shadow a house dog he installed a dog door for Shadow to access when he needed to step outside. Bebe didn’t work regular eight-hour shifts so he could be away too long for Shadow.

They dropped BJ off first at his school. Then Bebe had to travel to Kennedi’s school. Dropping BJ off first made him get there later than usual so he didn’t see the same parents he usually walked the halls with.

Up ahead the sight of a very shapely woman’s backside caught his attention. Damn, he thought. She was wearing a pair of black leggings with a red shirt that did nothing to cover up her voluptuous ass. Her long Senegalese twists cascaded down her back. Her ass was doing its own thing in those leggings like it wanted to be seen. Bebe watched each fat cheek bounce with every step she took.

“That’s Téa,” Kennedi said pointing to the little girl that walked alongside the big booty woman.

“Is she in your class?” Bebe asked.

“Yeah. We friends,” Kennedi said.

When Bebe made it to Kennedi’s class the woman was signing Téa in. Bebe couldn’t take his eyes off how amazing this woman’s body was. She finished signing the sign in sheet and accidentally bumped into Bebe.

“Oh, I’m sorry,” she said apologetically turning to face him.

It was the third week of the new school year. Why was he just now seeing her? She was peanut butter brown with sexy cognac-colored eyes. The front of her hair had been gathered and twisted up off her face neatly in a very sophisticated regal style. Her full lips formed an apologetic smile. Bebe noticed that her bottom lip had a cut in it like her mouth had hit up against her teeth.

"You're okay," he said. He added with a slight hint of flirtation, "I was standing too close anyway."

She blushed looking away.

Bebe found Téa's name. He looked at the signature beside it. Mikina Monroe. As he signed Kennedi in Ms. Nicole, Kennedi's teacher came up wearing a smile, "Good morning, Mr. Bebe."

"What's up?" Bebe threw at her.

Ms. Nicole gave him an incredulous look. "Really?"

Bebe stepped aside for the next parent. "What?"

"Are you always so blasé?" Ms. Nicole asked. She looked at Kennedi, "Sign in for me."

The big booty gem was leaving. Bebe gave Kennedi a hug and kiss, "Bye babygirl. Have a nice day, okay?"

Ms. Nicole, her assistant Ms. Yvonne, and two other mothers were looking at him with starry eyes and wearing smiles. *Let me get the hell up outta here*, Bebe thought.

Chapter 2

Miki thought Bebe was rather handsome. He had a thuggish quality about him though. The plain white tee, navy Dickies, and black workbooks looked good on him. His soft brown complexion was almost too smooth to go with such attire. His face was trimmed nicely to a thin mustache and a beard with a little length to it. He had deep-set brown eyes, thick eyebrows and long lashes. His lips were nicely shaped, not too full but not thin. And his hair! Again, the deep waves laying to his head did not match what he had on.

Miki watched him as he exited the door. He had to be a little over six feet or right at it. From the look of his toned forearms and the veins popping out Miki could conclude that he probably had a sexy body under that white t-shirt. She could see he had a bow to his legs and his left foot slightly crooked in as he walked. *How cute*, she thought. He was half pigeon-toed.

Miki took her foot off the brakes and slowly pulled out of her parking spot. A van was blocking her from exiting the lot. Bebe glanced back and saw her. Miki pretended not to see him and looked straight ahead. He had been heading to the curb where he and other parents parked alongside the road.

The van finally moved. As Miki eased her car forward Bebe got right in front of her car wearing a mischievous grin. Miki tried not to, but she smiled. He came around to her side. "What's up, beautiful?"

Miki noticed he had beautiful teeth. "Nothing."

"I want your name and your number and you're gonna

give 'em to me," he said playfully.

Miki replied, "And what if I don't?"

"Then I'll give you mine. Is that cool?"

"Do you not care if I have a man?"

Bebe shook his head, "Nope."

"Wow. You have no respect for the next man at all huh?"

Bebe said, "Let me keep it real with you. I have no respect for any man that did that to you. Or them love licks on your arms."

Miki flushed with embarrassment. A part of her felt ashamed but then she felt offended. How was he going to be tacky like that and point out her lip and the bruises on her arms?

"You too pretty of a woman to be getting hit on," Bebe continued. "Here, take my number. Call me when you want to be treated like a woman should be treated."

Miki said, "Don't worry about it. I won't call you."

"I tell you what. When you're ready you can find me here dropping off my daughter who happens to be in your daughter's room."

Miki offered him a sweet smile, "Okay Mr. Bebe."

Bebe looked at her suspiciously, "I didn't give you my name."

"Ms. Nicole said it," Miki said. A car had pulled up behind her.

Bebe looked at her, seduction playing in his eyes. "I'ma let you go. But I'll see you around."

Miki watched him saunter in front of her car towards the curb. He got in a navy older model Silverado truck. Her mind wandered dancing around with the idea of being with another man. It was times she wanted to be because everybody knew Redd had many girlfriends. Redd had a wife too that he swore up and down that he did not mess with.

Miki did have a fling with Kendrick, the one she recently got her ass beat about. He was during a time when Redd had violated parole and did nine months of time. That was a couple of years ago. Kendrick still had a thing for her. He was nice and a good friend but that was all Miki let it be.

Miki went in the opposite direction that Bebe's truck went, however she kept her eyes on it in the rearview mirror until it disappeared.

It was something about Bebe that grabbed her attention. He seemed very collected, confident, and somewhat cocky.

Miki found her way to Kat's condo. Kat had become Miki's best friend when they met some years ago. Miki was seventeen and Kat was nineteen. Kat was going with Redd's friend Oscar. They hooked up because they were always left alone together. Kat went through the same treatment from Oscar as Miki did with Redd. They talked about the two men behind their backs. When Miki was scared and needed someone to confide in, it was Kat and vice versa. Their friendship grew over the years.

"Getcho ass in here," Kat said holding the door open.

"I hope you made breakfast," Miki teased. She plopped down on Kat's ivory sofa. Kat's condo was decked out very chic and sexy. A person would think no children lived there but Kat had a nine-year-old daughter and a five-year-old son. Both were Oscar's.

"I don't cook. You should know that by now," Kat said going into the open kitchen. "But I got some frozen blueberry waffles and some sausage patties you can throw in the microwave."

"Girl, I'm good. I was just messing with you. I ate two boiled eggs for breakfast."

Kat gave Miki a blank look. "Two boiled eggs? I know you ain't trying that damn dieting shit again."

Miki grimaced, "I'm fat Kat."

"Where? The only thing about you that's fat is your booty. Stop playing."

"And my thighs...And my arms. Look at this," Miki said holding up her arm and wiggling it.

Kat sucked air through her teeth. "Ew Miki," she said with concern. She rushed over to her friend touching her arm where a purple whelp was. "He did this?"

Miki became self-conscious about it. "Yeah. It's fading now."

Kat frowned, "He gon' get his one day. You oughta beat him with a bat in his sleep. Crack him across the head on the first swing. That way he'd be so fucked up he won't be able to think when you swing that shit on him again."

Miki giggled, "Girl you crazy."

"I'm serious," Kat said. "Ox got one more damn time to try to put his hands on me. I'm sending that mothafucka right back to prison."

Miki sighed, "But why do we put up with this?"

Kat shrugged. She gestured around her condo, "This. The

way we live I guess. I can't think of another good reason why cause the dick sho' ain't all that."

"You ain't never lied," Miki said.

"I only let Ox come around for the money. Miki, you don't even work. Redd been taking care of you ever since you were seventeen. He put you in that big house and got you in a Range. You always dressed to the nines in designer shit. Hair laid...by me of course. Téa got the best shit. You live real good. Now you tell me why you ain't left."

Miki gave it some thought. "I'm scared."

"Fuck Redd!" Kat exclaimed. She got up and went back to the kitchen. "How many waffles you want?"

"I'm straight," Miki said sadly. Then she remembered Bebe and smiled. "Kat, this dude tried to talk to me at Téa's school."

"What he look like?"

"He was nice looking."

"Like how? Better than Redd?"

Miki didn't understand why but all of the ladies thought Montez Jeffries was the finest thing walking. Miki at one point thought so too but over the years he became uglier and uglier. He was mixed with sandy colored dreads and he had hazel green eyes. He was six feet and three inches tall with a large frame. He was solid but not cut up. Their daughter Téa had his eyes and his sandy hair.

Miki said, "Better than Redd."

"Ooh...better than Redd? Was he light skinned?"

"Nope. He's brown with a low cut but got waves for days

like the Pacific."

With a faraway look in her eyes, Kat pondered, "Hmmm...Chocolatey brother. If you had to compare him to somebody like a celebrity, who?"

"Uhm...I don't know," Miki answered.

"He's gotta look like somebody Miki," Kat said.

"He doesn't really. Not anybody we know. But remember how David Banner's beard used to be a lil long? That's how his is."

"So, you ain't gon' talk to him anyway," Kat teased.

"You're right. But the nigga had the nerves to say something about my bruises."

Kat snickered, "What did he say?"

"It doesn't matter. It was impolite like a child asking an amputee, 'hey what happen to yo hand'. He coulda act like he didn't see them."

"Everybody ain't you Miki. They can see the obvious when you pretend it doesn't exist."

It was almost two o clock when Bebe bothered to check his phone. "Shit," he hissed. He dialed his mother.

"What boy?" she answered.

"Mama, did you get Kennedi?"

"Yes. I been got her. Do I gotta get BJ too?" Joyce asked.

"Why you figure you gotta get BJ?" he asked confused.

"Cause Ken-Ken said Stefani brought him to you this morning."

"I don't know but he's in aftercare. I can call Stefani and ask."

"Blyss?"

"Yeah Mama."

"Can you check on your brother? Deja said she think he on that stuff again."

And do what? He knew his brother Silas was using. Shit, he never stopped. Bebe tried to get Silas on the right path time after time. He would straighten up for a couple of weeks then he'd disappear for a month or two until he needed something. Bebe didn't give him money freely. He made Silas put in a day's worth of labor with his landscaping and home improvement business.

"Oh, and your twin need you to call her."

"For what?"

"I think she need you to help her move."

"Where her nigga at?"

"Blyss, don't be like that. That's your sister. Bless needs your help."

"Alright Mama. Let me call Stefani real quick."

"Call me back to let me know either way."

Bebe hung up with his mother and dialed Stefani immediately. She didn't answer. He sent Bless a text: what you need?

He was about to text Stefani, but she called back. "Whatchu want?"

"Do I need to get BJ?"

“Nah, I got him. But can you get him Friday until Sunday night?”

“Uhm...this is my free weekend. I had him last weekend and the weekend before that...and the weekend before that one.”

“I know but Bebe, I’ve been invited to go to Vegas for the weekend,” she said excitedly.

“I’m sorry but am I supposed to be happy for you?” he asked sarcastically.

“Yes! I’ve never been.”

This right here...this was the shit he had to deal with. When it came to his children he did whatever he had to. If that meant putting his personal life aside, then so be it. But Stefani had to do better. “I’ll get him Stefani.”

“Thanks! Oh...and can I get five hundred dollars?”

Bebe hung up on her.

“Bebe, that lady said she didn’t want that red mulch,” Dinky said walking up on him.

“What she talking about? She asked for that.” Bebe said annoyed.

Dinky removed the toothpick from his mouth, “She said she wanted the dark mulch.”

“I hate dealing with her ass,” Bebe groaned. He walked back in the lady’s yard with Dinky. It took him ten minutes to convince the old white lady to go with the red mulch as initially ordered. He didn’t prefer it because it looked unnatural and it faded eventually. However, it could make a yard pop out. With her red shutters and white siding, the red mulch would look good. Today, this lady was getting red mulch because that's what she ordered.

Bebe called his mother back to inform her she didn't have to get BJ. Bless text back: I'm trying to move by this weekend. I need some help

Bebe text back: what day?

Bless: Saturday, in the morning

Bebe had his bank contracts to fulfill on Saturday mornings along with other commercial locations closed on the weekends. Bebe: how about I let u borrow my truck and Marvin can get somebody to help him move

Bless: Marvin ain't coming with me, he ain't helping

Bebe had to call her on that. When she answered Bebe shouted into the phone, "What!"

Bless laughed. "Shut up boy. You so retarded."

"What is this? You leaving that nigga?"

"I am. I got me a duplex for me and my two boys."

"Oh-oh! I get my twin back!"

"Bebe, stop that," she said. "So, can you help me?"

"Are y'all getting a divorce?"

"Right now I'm filing for a separation."

"Well, that's a start. I'll help you personally Saturday morning. And that mothafucka bet not trip either."

"He won't," she sighed. "I'm just tired of his stuff."

"Say 'shit' Bless. It sound better."

Bless giggled. "I will not use such language."

"You're so suburban. Where is this duplex?"

"It's close to your house actually. It's right there when you first turn into Northridge from Caruthers."

"I know what duplexes you're talking about. Shit, that's walking distance from me."

"Yep. Lil Marvin and Marcus will be bothering you every day."

"I wouldn't mind. I'm just glad to have you closer and away from dickface."

"Bebe. That's not nice."

"When it comes to niggas like him I don't have nothing nice to say. I met this girl this morning. Fine ass woman! But I recognized right away her dude had laid them hands on her. She had whelps on her forearms and her lip was cut. Just like you, she in a Range, one of the new ones. She was kept up real nice. I mean, is the luxury lifestyle really worth it?"

"When you're at that place in your life, for women like us it feels like it's worth it. But I'm at a different place now...I want real happiness," Bless said.

"I'm glad 'cause them boys don't need to see that shit."

"But you saw it Bebe. You came out alright."

"That coulda went either way though. Hell, I still suffered from anger issues."

"You're a good guy Bebe. The black community need more of you."

Bebe blushed. In his modesty he said, "Its other men out there that set a better example than I do."

"Why do you do that?"

"What?"

"You don't know how to take a compliment."

"I do Bless. It's just...I'm afraid I might fuck up at some point."

"You haven't in all these years. What you need is a good woman in your life. I'ma find you one...Down there at the church."

"Oh, hell nah! I'm good sis," Bebe exclaimed.

"I'ma hook you up," she sang.

"Hook your other brother up with some rehab." Bebe threw out.

Bless' tone changed to a sullen one. "Yeah, Mama told me about him. But what can we do Bebe?"

"I don't know," he sighed.

"What we won't do is totally give up on him. Right Bebe?"

"I guess," he said carelessly.

"Bebe!"

"Okay. We won't. Damn..."

Chapter 3

The rest of that week Miki secretly wished she accidentally bumped into Bebe. When she got to Téa's class, her friend Kennedi would already be there and his name, Blyss Blakemore, would be signed by Kennedi's. In the evenings, Kennedi would already be gone but there would be different signatures. Joyce Blakemore and Deja Blakemore. Miki wondered who those two women were.

"Miki!"

She snapped out of her daydream about Bebe. She looked over at Redd. "Huh?"

"What the fuck you over there thinking about?"

"Oh nothing." Miki said. "Is Alicia dropping Chanta off this weekend?"

"Nope. I told her we have plans," Redd said.

Miki smiled at him, "We?"

Redd smiled back, "Yeah, we. We going out."

"Where are we going?"

"Out," he said. He kissed her on the nose. He stood back and looked her up and down. "You slimming down. You look good. Keep it up."

Miki grinned. "You noticed."

"Uh-huh. Let me notice what it look like with you naked," he said sneakily.

"Téa is up," Miki whispered.

"She watching cartoons. C'mon, let's go upstairs real

quick," he suggested.

Miki led the way upstairs. They stopped briefly only to tell Téa that they would be right back.

Miki was eager to sex Redd. With all of his running around in the streets and overseeing his businesses their lovemaking had dwindled down to twice a week.

Miki remembered when Redd made her his side chic nine years before. Back then he was with Tamika. She thought she was going to take Raquel's place as wifey. Miki, at seventeen stole her spot. A few years later Miki was his number one. Although he was still married to Raquel she wasn't his wife. However, they never stopped fooling around. Miki knew Redd fooled with all of his baby mamas: Raquel, Tamika, Alicia and her.

Between the four of them he had six kids. His oldest was fifteen and his youngest was Téa at four. And nobody had him on child support.

Redd was a big-time drug dealer that laundered money through his businesses. He owned the barbershop/beauty shop Kings & Queens that Kat worked at. He also owned Club Envy, a popular urban nightclub. Then there were the two designer urban clothing stores, Black Elite and he partnered with Oscar in an auto audio/detail shop, M & M's. His paperwork was so clean the feds hadn't been able to touch him.

Redd was well known in the streets. Some loved him, others hated him. Women vied for his attention. Years ago, Miki felt like she had won the lottery when he noticed her at his cousin's basketball game. She had been on the step team. He was twenty-six and didn't care she wasn't entirely out of high school or the fact she was four months from turning eighteen.

He approached her, got her number, called, picked her up, took her out, took her back to his spot, fucked her and she's been Redd's girl since.

As Miki rode him she looked down at him and wondered what he thought of the cranberry bruises on her thighs, sides, and back. She could guess he was thinking she wouldn't have those bruises if she'd stop fucking with him.

Redd reached up and palmed her breasts. "You can ride the hell out of this dick baby."

Miki caught her bottom lip in between her teeth as she continued to work her body. He pulled her down holding her around the small of her back. They shared a deep kiss, but Miki didn't feel a connection. It didn't move her. She was just going through the motions pretending like it was the best sex she ever had. Bebe crossed her mind and she smiled. He looked like he could put it down in the bedroom with his sexy bow legs and slight pigeon toes.

Thinking of him Miki didn't realize Redd had come. Redd asked, "What the fuck you smiling for?"

Miki blushed, "Just feeling good."

Redd laughed. "Girl, get your goofy ass off me."

Miki moved aside so that Redd could get up. She laid there staring up at the ceiling. How could she talk to Bebe without being caught?

Miki and Kat found their way to their usual VIP seating. It wasn't really VIP, it was more like the owner's private suite.

Miki and Kat stood by the railing overlooking the dance floor.

Tonight, at Envy, The Lord's Wrath was having a biking party. There were all kinds of folks in the building showcasing their colors. Showing their colors was simply wearing their particular vests or armbands that represented their club. There had to be about twenty different bike clubs in there.

"I know he don't expect for you to stay up here all night," Kat said about Redd.

"You know how he is," Miki said.

"Let's go to the floor," Kat said pulling on Miki.

"Redd ain't gon' be mad at me."

"What I say the other day? Fuck that nigga! I bet he somewhere in some bitch face. All we tryna do is have fun."

It was easy for Kat to talk bold and brave; Oscar was on parole. He wasn't trying to get the police called on him no time soon. So, he wasn't laying hands on Kat like how he used to in the past. Redd wasn't on paper.

"Let's go," Kat said grabbing Miki's arm. They headed down the stairs to the main floor. Kat and Miki had to immediately start rejecting advances from guys who didn't know who they were.

A lot of people, especially within the biking crowd didn't see Miki. Redd rarely took Miki around this kind of crowd. She always graced his arm at a private party or something more formal.

The crowd was hyped and lively. Miki was stunned by some of the dancing going on. The ladies were taking twerking to another level. Then there was the way many of them were dressed. It was like they thought the least material they wore the flyer they were. They had on outfits that looked like monokinis.

Miki said, "Kat, what is this? Is this some type of freak party?"

"Girl naw. Folks just be ratchet," Kat said. "Let's dance."

Miki followed Kat to the dance floor. All she could hear was the usual catcalling.

"Hey girl!"

"Damn! You see her ass?"

"Ay, blue pants!"

"Lemme holla atcha."

"Got-damn!"

Men were so animalistic, Miki thought. No sense of discretion whatsoever.

Kat and Miki bumped into three more girls that ran in their circle on the floor. Mokeba, Kim, and Toya.

"What's up chicas!" Toya shrilled.

"What? Donnie let you out?" Miki teased.

"I can say the same about you. Where Redd?" Toya asked.

"That mothafucka prob'ly watching your ass on the cameras," Mokeba said.

Kat said, "You know what Miki? That's probably what they doing for real."

It was too late to run back to their section now. If he was mad now, he would still be mad if she went back. Miki said, "Oh well."

"We'll know in a minute," Mokeba said smacking her lips.

"I gotta get a drink. What about you Miki?" Kat said.

"I'm coming."

Chapter 4

Going out that night was worth it when Bebe saw Miki enter the club. She wasn't alone, so he assumed the guy with his hand securely around her back was her boyfriend. He also had to be the one that got physical with her.

Bebe watched them as they made their way to a private section separate even from VIP. Bebe had wondered what made them so special. He tapped his cousin Keonte. "Who that?"

"Who?" Keonte asked.

Bebe nodded up at the tiered level where Miki was. "Up there."

"That's Redd. He the owner of the club."

"He in a bike club?"

"Nah but he's affiliated with Ace of Spades. Like you; you affiliate with us, Lord's Wrath but you won't join. Nigga you got a bike and everything."

"I ain't got time for no club right now," Bebe said. "Who's the girl in the blue pants to him?"

"That's Miki, his woman. Don't be gettin' no ideas Bebe. Ain't nobody fighting at our party."

"I ain't gon' start nothing...Not here at least."

Keonte shot Bebe a contemptuous look. "Bebe, man, don't be going after her. Redd will have your ass killed over her. One of his other broads, he probably wouldn't care."

"Chill, wit'cho shaky ass," Bebe teased. He watched Redd

and the other guy leave the two women alone. They came downstairs and disappeared in the back. After about ten minutes Miki and her friend came down to the floor. They met up with three other girls and talked.

Miki was a sexy ass woman. Bebe observed how she along with her tall friend made heads turn. Her friend had wide hips and thick thighs which made her shapely, but her ass didn't stick out nice, thick, and meaty like Miki's ass in those blue pants. They were body hugging in every way. She wore a black fringed sleeve shirt that was high in the front and low in the back falling right at the hump of her ass. The shirt fringed along the bottom too. Her hair was still the same way when he saw her at the school. She appeared taller because of the black five-inch pumps she had on.

Miki and her friends walked over to the bar ordering drinks. Miki's back was to Bebe. Keonte looked at Bebe with his eyes locked on Miki. "Bebe!"

"I'll be back," Bebe said walking away.

"Nigga, I'm coming with yo stupid ass," Keonte said in exasperation.

Bebe squeezed in a spot right behind Miki. He had to brush up against her ass to order a drink. He said to the bartender, "Hennessy, no ice."

Miki glanced over shoulder with a frown and moved up.

Bebe said low to her, "You ain't gotta move beautiful."

Miki twisted around to see who he was. Her eyes widened, and she turned back to her friends. Bebe chuckled taking his drink. He leaned up against the bar with his back to it. He watched the crowd. He said, "I know you here with your man. So I ain't trying no shit. I'm just gonna stand here and enjoy the view."

Keonte laughed, "Man, you crazy!"

Miki seemed to relax. Her ass backed up against Bebe. She did it more than once. Then he felt her swaying, brushing his side.

Bebe chuckled and said lowly, "I hear you loud and clear."

Miki glanced back with a smile.

Bebe saw Redd in the distance. "Your man is coming."

Miki jumped away from him like he was on fire. She squeezed in the middle of her friends. That nigga had her extremely scared. That didn't sit well with Bebe.

"What are you doing?" the tall one asked. Then she looked Bebe's way and whispered something.

Redd and two of his cronies showed up at the bar. Redd glanced Bebe's and Keonte's way. "What's up Ke-lo," Redd said to Keonte. They exchanged a one-hand shoulder bump greeting.

Bebe sized Redd up. He was pretty sure he could kick Redd's ass, but Redd seemed like the type who wouldn't fight. He'd rather get somebody else to do it or use a gun.

Keonte said, "This my cousin Bebe. This is Redd."

Redd went to speak but Bebe casually walked away. He wasn't about to speak to Redd or get acquainted when he had every intention of getting his girl.

Miki was shocked by the disrespectful move Bebe just made. He was one arrogant man. But Miki had to admit, it was sexy as hell. The way he just walked away without a care in the world turned Miki on.

Redd asked Keonte, "The fuck his problem?"

Keonte said, "Sorry man, he a little tipsy. But he cool people."

"You betta check your cousin," Redd said with a threatening tone. Redd turned his attention back to Miki, "Why the fuck you down here?"

"We saw Free, Kim and Toya," Miki replied.

"I don't care who you saw. Barack and Michelle coulda been down here and if I ain't said you could come down here, then your ass can't be down here. C'mon."

Redd grabbed Miki by the wrist.

Mokeba whined, "Aw c'mon Redd. She can't hang out with us?"

"Nope," Redd said pulling Miki along.

Miki loudly said, "Redd, I got on these heels. You're gonna make me break my ankles!"

"They need to break. If they was broke you wouldn't be able to walk your ass down here."

Redd lead her back out the club through the back where his truck was. Miki asked, "Where are we going?"

"I'm taking you home."

"Why Redd?"

"You don't listen. You had all them niggas in there wanting your ass...Bringing you out is too stressful."

"How?"

"Cause Miki...it just is."

Redd took her back home, but he left right back out. She exhaled. Well at least he didn't hit her. As she removed her shoes her phone rang. It was Kat.

"What?"

"That nigga took you home didn't he?"

"Yep. And he left."

"What I wanna know is who was that fine ass dude that was talking to you? The one who ignored Redd. That shit was kinda funny."

"That's the dude I was talking about that tried to talk to me at Téa's school," Miki said excitedly.

"That's him?" Kat asked in disbelief.

"Yep. I guess he saw me. He sexy!"

"He can get it! So why won't you talk to him?"

"So Redd can beat his ass and mine?"

"Just talk to him. You ain't gotta have a relationship. Shit girl, that nigga got all kinds of hoes in his face. And he can dance. If you don't talk to him, I will. But I think he wants you."

"I don't know Kat." Miki heard a male ask Kat, "Who you talking to?"

Miki said, "Girl you go on and enjoy yourself. Ox gon' think you talking to some dude."

"Ox don't even need to be in my face. You heard what I did to her right. That bitch of his had the nerves to try to press charges on me but Ox talked her ass out of it. Now his ass tryna get some ass from me. Nigga still on fucking punishment."

Miki started giggling. "Girl you crazy."

"Alright. I'll hit you up tomorrow." Kat said before ending the call.

Miki went to sleep thinking of Bebe. He was different from all of the other guys that tried talking to her. He was confident, and Redd didn't intimidate him whatsoever. Miki liked that about him.

The next morning Miki got up and picked Téa up from Redd's sister house first thing. Miki got herself and Téa ready for church. Miki asked Redd, "Are you going with us?"

Redd mumbled, "Why you ask me that every Sunday?"

"Because I'm hoping you'll say yes one Sunday."

Redd flipped over on his back and looked at Miki and Téa. "My queen and my princess."

"Daddy, you the king!" Téa giggled.

"That's right baby. Daddy is the king," Redd grinned. "C'mere and give Daddy a hug."

Téa went around to his side of the bed. Redd hugged Téa to him. He looked at Miki. "Come here baby."

Miki went to his side. Redd kissed her on the lips. "I love you Miki."

"I love you too."

"I'm sorry."

"For?"

"Being so mean. I'm trying to work on it. Just continue to be patient with me."

Did he hear himself sometimes? Miki thought. She hated his apologies. They sounded genuine and sincere, but they were empty apologies. They weren't worth a penny. And what was up with this patient business? Be patient and in the meantime, accept the beatings while he's "working on it"?

Miki said, "Okay."

"Y'all go ahead and go. I'll meet y'all later at Mama's."

"Alright. Bye baby," Miki said. "C'mon Téa."

"Bye Daddy," Téa said sweetly.

Miki met up with her mama Ava and stepdaddy Larry at the church. Her older sister Maddie, her husband Gary, and their three kids joined them too.

Maddie leaned over the pew and said to Miki, "I need to have a word with you."

Miki looked over her shoulder. Maddie had her head down pecking away on her cellphone. She briefly stopped only to push her glasses up on her nose. Maddie was older than Miki by seven years. They had a sister in between them, Kizzie. Maddie was the sensible mature one. She had the husband, the kids, the dogs, picket fence, the house, and a career. She actually owned a catering business specializing in bakery and pastries. She was in the process of opening her own store. She recently ventured into writing also. Her husband had a great job as a computer software engineer.

"What about?" Miki asked.

"We'll talk after service," Madison said still not looking up from her phone.

"Where is Kizzie?" Miki asked.

Ava said, "She should be on her way."

Miki sat back relaxed as service was about to begin. She let her eyes wander over the congregation. She spotted her favorite people to watch down front. Miki didn't know what it was, but she found Abe Masters and his brothers to be the sexiest men she had ever laid eyes on. They were a beautiful. And that damn Abe was dreamy with his icy blue eyes. She could stare at him all day.

Kizzie snuck in during the recital of the mission statement. Her girlfriend accompanied her. Ava scoffed at the sight of Toni. Miki shot her mother the side eye look, then turned to Kizzie and Toni with a smile. "Glad you made it."

Kizzie tugged Miki's twists. "I love your hair."

Miki said, "Thanks." She looked at her sister's dreads that were almost as long as Miki's twists. Kizzie had them bleach blonde and they really stood out. Kizzie was a fem but in an eccentric way. She had a funky urban hippie appeal. Toni on the other hand was a stud all the way. Short boy haircut, plaid button-down shirts with khaki pants. She was somewhat boyishly handsome.

As a family they enjoyed service together listening to Pastor Thomas. It was a good one as always. As soon as it was over Maddie pulled Miki and Kizzie aside. "Okay, listen up. Mama and Larry's ten-year anniversary is coming up. I wanna throw them a nice surprise party. What say you?"

"Is this what you needed to have a word about with me?" Miki asked.

"Yeah. I couldn't say it with Mama next to you," Maddie said.

"What do you need us to do?" Kizzie asked.

"Well that's what I wanted to go over with y'all about. Let's make it a date. I gotta get with Debra too. She will be vital to the whole setup. So, what's a good time for y'all to meet? We can have dinner, lunch, and go out for drinks."

Kizzie said thoughtfully, "You know that would be a good idea. Cause how often do we get to get together anymore?"

"Exactly," Maddie said. She grinned wrapping either arm around her sisters. "I miss you guys."

Miki said, "You're the busy one. And you Kizzie are all over the place."

"Let's do dinner this weekend," Kizzie suggested.

Maddie asked Miki, "Do I have to go to Redd for permission?"

"You're not funny," Miki said blankly.

"I'm just saying. You know how he can be," Maddie said shaking her head.

"Yeah, I know, but I'll be there," Miki assured her.

Ava walked over gracefully, "What are you three over here whispering about?"

"Nothing Mama," Kizzie smiled. "Mama, you're looking good. Whatchu doing different?"

Ava smiled proudly, "Well if you must know, I've lost fifteen pounds."

"Larry must be getting it in again," Kizzie teased.

Maddie looked at Kizzie scornfully, "Seriously Kizzie? We're still on church grounds."

Ava quipped, "That too."

"Ew! Mama," Miki laughed with Kizzie. Maddie shook her

head in shame.

Miki said her goodbyes and gave them all hugs and kisses. As she sat in her car an exciting feeling came over her. It was Sunday. Monday was the next day. She would purposely run into Bebe.

Chapter 5

Since Bebe had BJ Monday morning, he ran behind dropping Kennedi off. He didn't mind because he was hoping to bump into Miki. He couldn't wait to see her face again. All Bebe could think about was the feel of her ass brushing up against him Saturday night at the club.

Even though he didn't mind having to drop off BJ, Bebe was still upset with Stefani. She was supposed to get BJ upon her return. She called him late the night before and told Bebe she was tired.

When Bebe signed Kennedi in he was a little disappointed to see Miki had already signed Téa in. She signed in at ten minutes after eight. It was now a quarter "til nine. Bebe looked and saw the little sandy hair green eyed girl happily greet Kennedi with a hug. Téa was definitely Redd's daughter.

When Bebe headed towards his truck he was pleasantly surprised. A huge grin grew across his face. Miki was in her white Range blocking him in. She smiled when she saw him approach.

"Have you been waiting on me?" Bebe asked.

"Nah, I just like hanging around in the parking lot of schools," Miki said sarcastically.

"I feel special," Bebe smiled. "So what's up?"

Miki gave it some thought. "I'm not sure...but I think I want that number now."

"I know you do. Your ass told me that Saturday night." Bebe pulled out his cellphone. "What's your number?"

Miki called it out. Bebe called her so that she could have his. Miki tapped around on her phone. She turned her screen to him. "You're Ms. Brenda."

Bebe chuckled, "Really?"

Miki giggled, "Yeah."

Bebe admired her smile. Her whiskey-colored eyes sparkled. He said, "You're pretty Miki. You deserve to smile like this all the time."

Miki blushed and did a half shrug. "Yeah...well you know my situation. You wanna deal with that?"

"Oh I'm taking you from that nigga," Bebe said with confidence.

"Is that so?"

"It is."

"Hmm...How do you plan on doing that?"

"I'm a man about action. I hate talking about what I will do, what I can do or what I wish I could do. I just do it and let my actions speak for me."

"Okay," Miki said plainly. She smiled and said, "Well Ms. Brenda, I gotta go."

Bebe laughed. He asked, "When can I call you?"

"Anytime between nine and six I guess but Ms. Brenda works here at the school. Remember that."

"I got it beautiful. You be careful and have a good rest of the day."

"I will. You the same."

Bebe didn't use Miki's number right away. He waited and

wanted to see how serious she was. If she was really interested in him she would contact him. Usually Bebe didn't operate like that. He liked doing the chasing. But this situation was different. If he was going to pursue Miki she had to be as interested in him as he was in her.

The whole week went by and nothing from Miki. Bebe was somewhat disappointed. Redd either had her scared to death or she didn't think Bebe was worth it.

"Whatchu getting into tonight?" Dinky asked. It was Saturday and the day's work was complete. They were returning equipment back to Bebe's office and garage.

Bebe joked, "I wish I could get into some pussy."

"And you can't?" asked Ricky.

"Nigga, you got all kinds of bitches throwing pussy at you," Wallace exclaimed. He was an older man that Bebe took a chance on by employing him. In the two years Wallace had been working for Bebe he backslide twice at the beginning. He was an alcoholic and his family had turn their backs on him. He got his stuff straight and cut out hard liquor. He had a beer from time to time, but Wallace didn't want to return to what he was. He had his family back and a steady job with Bebe.

"They having something down at The Cut," Dinky said.

"I gotta get a babysitter," Bebe said.

"Where Auntie Joyce?" Dinky asked.

"She gone to the casino with the rest of them old biddies," Bebe answered. "I can probably ask Bless. I know Deja already got plans."

"You got BJ too?" Ricky asked.

Bebe had his eyes on Chris and Enrico trying to back a

trailer into the garage. "Yeah I got BJ. I had him until Tuesday then Stefani put him back on me this morning."

"He might as well live with you," Dinky stated.

"Stefani ain't gonna do that," Bebe murmured. "Somebody go help dumb and dumber 'fore they tear up my shit."

"Chris and his non-driving ass," Ricky grumbled under his breath as he headed towards the two men.

Bebe's phone vibrated in his pocket. He removed it to see there was a text notification. He opened his messages.

Beautiful: Hey Ms. Brenda, this Miki. Having a meeting tonight @ 7 at Logan's for surprise party planning of Ava's and Larry's 10th yr anniversary. Ur welcome to come...Hope to see u there!

Huh? Did she mean to send that to him? Did she forget she put his number under Ms. Brenda?

Bebe text back: Which Logan's?

Beautiful: Oops...sorry...the Northridge one

Bebe: ...and I just show up?

Beautiful: ask for the Monroe party

Bebe: tonite?

Beautiful: Ms. Brenda? U in the first stages of senile dementia?

Bebe: I get confused sweetie...and I'm not that damn old but old enough to throw you over my lap and spank that ass!

Beautiful: lol...we'll see about that...

Bebe: see u at 7

Bebe was grinning from ear to ear.

“Who you texting got you cheesing so hard?” Dinky asked.

“That girl I was telling you about,” Bebe said. He checked the time. He had two hours to get cleaned up, dressed, and to the restaurant. “Dinky, lock up the shop for me. I gotta go.”

Once in his truck Bebe called Bless. “Sis, can the kids please stay overnight? I’ll bring them a change of clothes.”

“I guess. What is it?”

“The girl from Kennedi’s school. I’m meeting her in two hours.”

“This a date?”

“I guess.”

“Well okay brother. They’re here already and I don’t mind.”

“Thanks. Love you.”

Miki knew she was taking a chance, but she had to see Bebe. Redd had been home damn near every day that week. He said he was sick. All he wanted Miki to do was cater to him. She was glad Bebe hadn’t called her, but she didn’t want him thinking she wasn’t interested.

Miki had Maddie to pick her up from home in front of Redd who was now miraculously well since it was Saturday. Redd was dropping Téa, Chanta, and Montrell off at his mother’s house to spend the night. Maddie went on a rant about Redd never letting Miki spend time with her sisters. Maddie assured him she would keep her safe and return Miki home at a decent hour.

Redd relented only after putting his emphasis on the

stipulations. He told Miki to be home by eleven-thirty and he wanted her to call him to let him know she was in the house. She couldn't drink nor smoke. He made her wear denim capris with a tunic tee and tennis shoes. That was his way of making Miki less...attractive. She thought it was dumb because no matter what she put on her ass was always going to be evident.

Miki didn't care. If it would make Redd less worried about what she was doing then fine. Besides it seemed like Redd was eager to get somewhere himself.

Miki suggested the Northridge area because it was where Maddie lived, and Redd didn't do business in that area. Northridge was a middle-class area with a diverse race of people. It was nice. Miki wanted to get a house there, but Redd thought the three thousand square foot house he bought was a steal compared to the price for a house like that in Northridge.

Miki sat down at the table with Maddie, Kizzie, Toni and Maddie's friend and worker Tanya. She lowered her voice, "Y'all I have to confess something."

"What?" Maddie asked.

"I know I'm supposed to be here to help plan Mama's anniversary party, but I used this girl's thing as a front. Thank you, Maddie because you helped me without knowing you were helping me."

Maddie was confused, "I'm lost."

"Mikina! I know you ain't about to abandon us to be with someone else," Kizzie said with surprise.

"I am... Sorry," Miki said sheepishly.

Maddie grinned wickedly, "So you've been holding out on us. You've met someone."

Miki looked at the time on her phone. It read 6:56. “Yeah. And I’ve never done this before. I mean I was seeing Kendrick, but Redd was behind bars.”

“Well you know how I feel about Redd,” Kizzie said turning up her nose.

Tanya said, “You ain’t his wife.”

“Right,” Kizzie agreed.

“And we all know Redd spreads himself thin,” Maddie said. She sighed heavily. “Just be careful Miki.”

“Who’s this guy you’re being risky for?” Kizzie asked.

“He should be coming through that door at any time,” Miki said looking toward the front of the restaurant. “So, this is what we’re gonna do. While y’all eat and plan I will be over there with him.”

“Okay,” Kizzie said.

Tanya asked, “Is that him?”

The ladies twisted around and partially stood to get a look. Miki smiled, “It is.”

Bebe followed the hostess to their reserved table. He was clean like he had been at Envy. However, he was more casual. The orange Trukfit t-shirt he had on complimented the brown of his skin. The logo had camouflage in it that matched the camouflage cargo pants he wore. On his feet looked like a fresh pair of Air Max that were dark green with white Nike logo and orange soles.

“Damn!” Maddie breathed. “He’s a hottie Miki.”

“I know him,” Toni grinned. “That’s Bebe. He’s my cousin’s cousin.”

"What can you tell me about him?" Miki asked.

"He's cool people," Toni said. She laughed. "Don't worry girl. If Redd is as bad as I've heard, then Bebe will be like a breath of fresh air. Trust me."

"Okay. Well I'm gone," Miki said. She made her way to the table.

Bebe looked up at her and smiled. "Hey beautiful."

"Hey," she said as she sat across from him. "I'm glad you were able to come on such short notice."

"You coulda text me ten minutes ago and I still would have made it here just to see you," he said sweetly.

Their waitress came to take their orders for drinks.

"Are you driving or something?" Bebe asked.

"No. I rode with my sister. Why?"

"Because you didn't get an alcoholic drink."

"Oh, I can't...well he doesn't like for me to drink when I'm not in his company," she explained.

"Ain't that some shit," Bebe mumbled. He said, "You know I don't like him, right?"

"I gather that," Miki said.

Bebe studied the menu while saying, "I think I'ma have to kick his ass one day."

"I would hope it wouldn't come to that."

"With a bitch like him? Oh, it's gonna happen."

"Bebe, why are you so willing to fight for me, and you barely know me?"

Bebe placed the menu down and looked into her eyes. "Miki, I'm a passionate person. And one of my biggest passions is hating niggas like him."

"Is there something personal there?"

"There is."

"A relative?"

"My mama and my twin sister."

Miki asked excitedly, "You're a twin?"

"Yeah."

"What's her name?"

"Bless. I'm Blyss."

"That's different. I like that. Do she act like you?"

Bebe chuckled, "And how do I act?"

"Kinda arrogant."

Bebe laughed as the waitress returned with their drinks. She was ready to take their food orders. After she left Bebe asked, "How old are you?"

"Twenty-six. You?"

"Thirty-three."

"No, you're not," Miki said in disbelief.

"Do I need to take out my license? How old did you think I was?"

"My age."

"Seven years isn't too much of a difference. We were born in the same decade."

"But you're in your thirties. You look so young. Is Kennedi

your only child?"

"I have a six-year-old son named BJ. What about you?"

"Téa is my only child."

"Do you want more?"

"One day. I wanna be married."

"You're not married to him?" Bebe asked incredulously. He looked at the diamond solitaire on Miki's left ring finger.

Miki looked down at the ring. She said, "He gotta get a divorce to marry me."

"He's married?"

Miki nodded.

Bebe gave a sinister laugh. "I'm really about to take your ass from him now."

Miki looked over at her sisters and friends. She giggled because they were staring and being silly.

Bebe looked in the direction she was gazing. He caught them staring then pretending like they were never looking his and Miki's way. "Who are they?"

"The one in the glasses and the one with the blonde dreads are my two sisters. The one beside my sister with the glasses is one of her close friends. And the one beside my sister with the dreads is—"

"Toni. I know her. Your sister a lesbian?"

"Toni's her dude," Miki answered.

Bebe grinned at Toni and shouted, "What's up kinfolk?"

Oh my God, Miki thought, *he's ghetto and country*. She laughed, "Bebe, you got people looking over here."

"So."

"You're crazy."

"Naw, I'm very sane. But I tell you what might push me towards insane."

"What?"

He grinned slyly, "I can't tell ya."

"Uh! You play too much."

Bebe stared at her long and she wondered what he was thinking about. He smiled and said, "I think I just found Mrs. Bebe Blakemore."

———

Since they were in the Northridge area, Bebe's house wasn't too far. They discovered that Maddie's house was just two streets over from Bebe.

It was Miki's suggestion to go back to his place. She seemed a bit surprised when Bebe told her he had his own home where he lived with his two kids. Most women were surprised. Bebe wasn't a bullshitter and he was about his business. He didn't feel a need to impress people and live by their standards. If they didn't like him how he was then fuck 'em. And Bebe lived by his own rules.

Being analytical and with substance Bebe tried to live smart. He wasn't frivolous with his money. He would splurge and indulge in something pricey every now and then, but it wasn't often. Investing in home ownership was necessary for Bebe. It was what he wanted his kids to have. Bebe specifically picked Northridge to purchase his home. It was a beautiful area and the people cared about their property.

Miki looked around in the living room and over to the right at the formal dining room. She said, "Nice house."

"Yeah, I haven't really taken the time to furnish every room in here though," he said nodding towards the empty dining room. "I'm not in a hurry."

"It's still nice," Miki said walking further into the living room.

Shadow came running in from outside. Miki shrieked and ran for the front door. Bebe laughed. "He won't hurt you."

"I don't like dogs!" She was clutching the front doorknob.

Shadow jumped up on Bebe happy to see him. Bebe pushed him away, "Get off me. You see I have company. And what was your ass doing outside?"

Shadow went to smell Miki. She said, "Will he bite?"

"Nah. He's the goofiest Rottweiler Doberman mixed dog I've ever seen. Him and Kennedi are close. Partners in crime."

Miki was still nervous. Bebe reached out for her. "C'mon, he won't bite. He'll leave us alone in a minute."

Miki walked behind Bebe with her eyes on Shadow watching his every move.

"Let me show you around," Bebe said pulling her along.

After a while Miki relaxed and was adjusting to Shadow's presence. He was a friendly dog. He was goofy like Bebe said. Shadow liked sliding across the hardwood floors.

Bebe showed her his bedroom which was untidy. He said, "Why make up my bed if I'm gonna mess it right back up?"

He showed her the mudroom and laundry room. They walked through the kitchen. Miki asked if he could cook. Of course, he boasted about being an excellent cook. Around the back of the kitchen was a sunken sunroom currently being used as a recreational room. A door in the hallway lead downstairs to a den. On the left side of the house were the three secondary bedrooms and two full baths. One of the rooms was Bebe's home office.

Miki said, "I really love this house."

"I do too. That's why I bought it," Bebe said smugly.

Miki rolled her eyes playfully.

"So...," Bebe started.

Miki raised her eyebrows, "So?"

"How much time do we have?" Bebe asked.

"About two hours," Miki said.

Bebe casually said, "There's a lot we can do in two hours."

Miki grinned sneakily. "Like what?"

"Why do I sense you wanna be a bad girl?" Bebe asked suspiciously.

"I don't. I was just wondering what you had in mind," She said innocently.

"Not standing here."

"Well let's sit down."

"I was thinking lay...lay down...in my bed," Bebe joked.

Miki shot him a look.

Bebe changed his tone to a serious one. "I'm just playing. You don't have to do anything you don't wanna do."

Miki said quietly, "I want to. I just don't wanna do it for

the wrong reasons."

"Like get back at him?"

"Yeah. I'm attracted to you. I feel comfortable with you. I like you. But..."

"There is no but. That's enough to not be doing it for the wrong reasons," he said pulling her close to him.

Miki held onto him by his biceps as his arms embraced her. She looked up at him and whispered, "I'm scared."

"Of being with another man?"

"No. I'm scared of Redd."

Bebe released her from his hold and took her by the hand. "C'mon...let me make you forget about him for two hours."

Miki didn't object nor resist as Bebe pulled her into his bedroom. He ordered her to sit on his bed. In a slow tender and careful manner, Bebe removed her shoes and her socks. He gently massaged her feet. Miki hadn't never had her feet massaged by a man. It felt wonderful. Her mouth fell open when Bebe kissed her toes. Oh my God! *What is-h—Shit, that feel good*, Miki thought.

Bebe continued to massage up her leg until he got to her waistband. He unbuttoned and unzipped her Capri pants. Those were tugged off. In the dim lighting Bebe could still see the fading bruises. Damn, what did he do to her? Bebe wanted to know but he didn't want to ruin the moment. Instead he caressed and kissed her in all the bruised areas of her thick thighs. He looked up at her. She had one side of her bottom lip caught between her teeth anticipating his next move.

Bebe brought his mouth to hers in a deep sensual kiss assaulting her tongue immediately. Miki returned the kiss as her pussy throbbed. Her hands started roaming up under Bebe's shirt. And just as she thought, he was ripped. He was also sensitive on the lower flanks of his sides. Her hands caressed him there and he grabbed them. When she tried again he groaned and snatched her hands from him and ravenously attacked her neck with hungry kisses.

Bebe's hand went under her shirt around her back. He unfastened her bra. He pulled away so that he could ease her shirt over her head.

When he stood Miki could see that his dick was pressed hard against the inside of his pants. Miki removed her bra, slung it to the floor and grabbed his dick. Bebe stood fully before her looking down at her. He asked, "Whatchu gon' do wit dat?"

Miki couldn't contain her smile. She thought he was so sexy and cute at the same time. Miki took her time the same as he had done, to unfasten his pants. She reached in his boxer briefs and took him in her hand. She felt him jump upon her touch. She pulled his dick out and stroked it, getting acquainted with it, admiring it. He had girth and if she had to guess he was a good nine inches in length. It seeped pre-cum. Miki rubbed it in with the tip of her tongue encircling his head.

Her name escaped his lips in a whisper. "Miki..." he moaned.

Miki licked down one side of shaft then sucked his head. She did the opposite side then sucked his head. She repeated it for the top and bottom until he was lubricated in her saliva before taking him in her mouth.

Bebe wanted to cry she was sucking him that good. She was very methodical and deliberate with her technique. She would suck with the right amount of suction in a twisting motion using no hands. Her hands gripped him by the hips keeping everything in place. Every now and then she would deep throat him balls deep. Jesus! Bebe grabbed her twists and yanked her head back. “Damn girl! What the fuck you doing?”

Confused by his angry expression she asked, “You didn’t like it?”

“Hell yeah I liked it but you tryna get a nigga crazy over yo ass already. Getcho ass up in the bed!”

Miki giggled as she scooted back against his pillows. She slid off her panties and tossed them. She watched Bebe remove his clothing. His dick stood straight out. She smiled at the sight of his naked body. He was very nice to look at. It was odd to see a man nowadays without at least one tattoo. Bebe had none.

Bebe crawled in the bed covering her body with his. He aggressively kissed her in a possessive way claiming her as his in the moment. With the same passion he left kisses down her neck, over her shoulders, to her breasts where he suckled both with the same amount of attention, and on down over her taut stomach. As he kissed her stomach Bebe knew he had plans to put a baby in there one day.

When he reached the neatly edged triangle of hair in between her hips he stopped. Miki looked down at him with question. He said, “I don’t eat pussy.”

“Nigga! You gonna eat mine tonight!” Miki said playfully but she was serious.

“Damn, it’s like that?” Bebe asked. His voice softened, “Spread your pussy open for me.”

Miki widened her legs and reached down to do as he said. Bebe lowered his head in between her thighs. With the tip of his tongue he tickled her clit. Miki inhaled and caught her breath. His lips closed around her clit as he gently sucked it. Miki gasped without releasing the first breath. Then his tongue caressed every inch, every fold of her pussy back up to her clit. Miki had moved her hands away and they were now on his head as she wiggled under him thrusting back against his tongue. He then inserted it into her opening and tongue-fucked the shit out of her.

Don't eat pussy my ass! Miki thought as his tongue found its way back to her clit. He stayed on it beating it with his tongue. Miki's breathing deepened as she felt herself climaxing, "Oh Bebe...baby...I'm about to cum... Oh shit!"

Miki thrust wildly holding Bebe's head in place as her pussy walls convulsed. His tongue was still applying pressure on her engorged now very sensitive clit. Not able to bear anymore Miki pushed his head away and clamped her legs tight.

"Goddamn, you pushing on a nigga," Bebe mumbled.

Miki half whimpered half giggled as she came down off her orgasmic high. Bebe positioned himself in between her legs and kissed her with her juices on his lips, mustache and on his chin. Miki kissed him wildly inhaling the scent of her.

The tip of his dick found her wet opening. Miki thrust upward to have him inside her. When Bebe felt the warmness of her around his head he wanted to push deep inside, but he told himself about not being responsible when it came to pussy. He was disciplined in all other aspects of his life except when it came to pussy.

"C'mon baby," Miki whispered.

"Wait," he said. He retrieved a condom from his nightstand.

Miki wouldn't object. Shit, she should make Redd wear condoms, but she knew that was out of the question.

On his haunches Bebe held her legs open and entered her. He knew Miki had sex with Redd on a regular basis, but her pussy was resistant at first. Her walls gave in and received him wrapping around him snugly. "Damn baby...whatchu doing with this tight ass pussy?"

He didn't really want her to answer that. He lowered himself over her and covered her mouth with his. She moaned under him as he stroked her at an even pace. He pushed her legs up for deeper penetration. Miki cried out and pushed on his hips.

He moved her hands and began pounding inside her. Her moans and cries got louder. "Bebe baby...Oh God! Shit!"

The sound of his thighs slapping the back of hers drowned out the wet sloshing sound her pussy was making as she continued to excrete her juices. Miki tried to push him away and lower her legs. Bebe wouldn't let her at least not right away. He pummeled deep inside. He wanted her to feel all of him, so it was him she only thought about.

Miki screamed, and her walls tried to expel Bebe as her pussy violently convulsed around him. Gripping him like that caused Bebe to release sooner than he intended. "Shit...damn, damn shit! Miki baby...what did you just do?"

"I don't know...," she whimpered.

Bebe eased out of her. She was wet, and he was covered in

her wetness. There was even a wet spot under her. "Did you just pee in my bed?"

Miki sat up to look under her. "Did I?"

Bebe chuckled and kissed her tenderly on the lips. "No goofy ass girl."

Miki looked into his eyes when he pulled away. She wished it was Bebe she could fall asleep with that night.

"What?" he asked.

Miki shook her head and looked away.

Bebe removed the condom and tossed it. He laid down beside Miki. "Come here."

Miki snuggled in his arms. "How much time do we have left?"

"I'll get you back to your sister in time. Don't think about that just lay right here with me," Bebe said.

Miki was about to relax when her phone started ringing from her pants. Miki jumped up and went to the edge of the bed frantically searching for her phone. She got in time to answer. "Hello?"

"Hey baby," Redd said.

"Hey," she said trying to remain cool.

Bebe knew she had to be talking to Redd because she got nervous. As she spoke her ass was in the air. Bebe could see her pussy and started getting aroused again. He found himself stroking himself then realized he didn't need to stroke himself when he had pussy right in front of him. He reached over and got another condom.

Miki said, "Yeah, I'll be home in about thirty minutes."

"Don't forget to call me Miki. I ain't playing."

"I won't," she said. Miki closed her eyes as she felt Bebe enter her from behind.

"It's too late for you to be out as it is," Redd said.

Miki didn't say anything. Bebe was long stroking her hitting bottom. It had her trembling.

"You hear me Miki?" Redd asked.

"Yes," Miki said trying to keep her voice even. "Redd, let me catch..." she paused as Bebe knocked her forward. "...up with my sister...I'll call you as soon as I...get in the house."

"Okay. Love you baby."

"I love you too." Miki hung up. Bebe didn't give her a chance to confront him. He started pounding in her relentlessly. It was too much. Miki collapsed on the bed trying to get away from him. Bebe fell on top of her grinding his dick in her.

Miki cut her eyes back at him and laughed softly. Bebe whispered in her ear, "You know you done fucked up."

Yes, Miki knew she had just made things complicated. When she told Bebe she didn't want to have sex with him for the wrong reasons a part of her wanted to be with him just because Redd slept around. She thought after it was over she would be able to make it a one-time thing and conclude it was a mistake. She would walk away still feeling empty. But that's not how she felt at all.

"Call me or text me tomorrow okay?" Bebe said.

Miki nodded. He took her hand in his and brought it up to

his lips. He said, "I really don't want to let you go."

"I know," Miki said quietly. She leaned over and kissed him softly on his lips. "I gotta go. But I'll talk to you tomorrow."

Bebe didn't say anything. He watched her ease out of his truck and shut the door. He kept his eyes on her. The front door opened.

Miki turned around and waved at him. She didn't step inside the house until his truck was out of sight.

Miki shut the door behind her and fell against it. "Ah! Oh my God! Maddie, what have I done?"

"Did you sleep with him?" Maddie asked.

"Yes!"

Kizzie walked into the foyer, "Did I hear correctly?"

"If you heard that I slept with him then yeah, you heard right," Miki said.

"Was it good?" Tanya asked from the kitchen.

Miki walked toward the kitchen. "It was great!"

"I can't believe this," Kizzie teased. "You creeping on Redd."

"She should just leave his ass," Tanya said under her breath.

Miki looked at the time on Maddie's wall clock. "Is that the right time?"

"Yeah, give or take a few minutes. You need to get home?" Maddie asked.

Miki smelled her clothes. "I need to take a shower. I smell

like Bebe."

"Well let's get you home," Maddie mumbled.

"Wait, I want details," Tanya interjected.

"Ooh, Tanya, I can't. Bebe special," Miki said playfully.

"Special my ass! Spill it."

"Ride with me and she can fill you in on the way to her house," Maddie said. "You coming Kizzie?"

"I gotta wait on Toni, remember?" Kizzie said. She helped herself to a homemade snickerdoodle. "You won't have no cookies when you get back."

Miki snatched one from the tray. "You make these Maddie?"

"Uh...yeah," Maddie said grabbing her keys.

"I thought you were dieting," Kizzie mentioned.

Miki said, "Forget a damn diet."

As soon as Miki got in the house she drew her a bath. She called Redd. He didn't answer. She left him a voicemail message and sent him a text.

Miki eased into the tub and immediately her mind was flooded with thoughts of Bebe. She smiled. When she thought of him pounding her it sent electricity through her body and made her shudder. "Ooh...damn."

Her phone alerted her to a text message received. It was Redd responding. She reached over the tub for her phone. She grinned. Ms. Brenda: Had a good time, glad u invited me

Miki replied: glad u did, can't wait until the actual party

Ms. Brenda: me either...g'nite

Miki smiled: good night

Miki finished her bath. She went to sleep wearing a smile.

"Miki."

"Huh?" Miki mumbled. She was sleeping good when Redd came in waking her.

"Baby, who is this Ms. Brenda?"

Miki's heartbeat quickened. Her eyes opened. Redd was on the side of the bed going through her phone.

"Oh, she's a teacher at Téa's school. Her and Mama are good friends," Miki answered. She closed her eyes and turned over on her back.

"So she helping with the party?"

"Yeah. What time is it?"

Redd put her phone down. "It ain't two yet."

Miki drifted back off to sleep.

"Why you so tired?"

Her eyes opened again. "Huh?"

"You wasn't drinking was you?"

"Uh-uh. I ate too much though. We had a good time. And you know my sister is crazy."

"You still watching what you eat right? Your thighs getting real thick."

Bebe love my thighs, Miki thought to herself.

"I ate chicken and a salad. Then I stuffed my mouth with some sausage. I know I shouldn't have but it was so good!" Miki said. She giggled thinking of her time with Bebe. He was the best sausage she ever tasted.

"Well you can cheat every now and then."

"Sausage ain't really cheating. I'm on a low carb diet so I can have meat."

Redd grabbed himself and joked, "You want some of this meat?"

I've been talking about that kind of meat the whole time...just not yours, Miki thought. "You crazy."

Miki was disappointed when she realized Monday was a holiday. It totally slipped her mind it was Labor Day. That meant she would have to wait until Tuesday to see Bebe again.

In church she text Bebe through the whole service. She deleted all of it because they were talking about what they were going to do to each other the next time. She felt a little guilty because she was lusting and fornicating in her head right there in church.

Bebe wanted to see her again. He asked to see her Tuesday. Miki didn't know how she could, but she wanted to see him just as bad.

Chapter 6

Miki wasn't in the mood for accompanying Redd to one of his friend's house for the holiday. He insisted she come along. The only good thing was Kat and Toya would be there.

"What's wrong Miki?" Kat asked bringing her red cup up to her mouth.

"Nothing," Miki said sadly. She kept her eyes on Redd as he clowned with the other guys.

"What he do?"

"Made me come here, for one," Miki retorted.

"You don't wanna be here?" Kat asked.

"I'd rather be at my sister's."

"Then what would I do? Ain't none of these bitches here my friend except Toya. And if that bug-eyed Powder looking hoe over there with Ox don't stop watching me I'ma have to pop her in the throat. I can't help it Toya invited me. Toya don't know her."

Miki snickered. She looked around the backyard. "Where my children at?"

"I think they all went inside."

Miki leaned in closer to Kat and whispered, "I need to tell you something."

"What?"

"I saw Bebe."

Kat gasped then grinned. "When?"

"Saturday night."

"Heifa, it's Monday. Two days and you just now telling me?"

"I couldn't tell you yesterday because Redd was home."

Eager to hear more Kat asked, "Well?"

"It was good."

Kat fell out in disbelief. "Nah bitch! Oh shit! Miki!"

Miki tried to get Kat to be quiet as she had drawn attention their way.

Kat whispered sneakily, "You fucked him?"

Miki nodded with a guilty grin.

Kat fell out again in disbelief. "I ain't believing this shit!"

"Will you be quiet," Miki hissed. Redd cut his eyes their way.

"Okay. I'm sorry," Kat breathed. She whispered, "You gon' see him again?"

"He wanna see me tomorrow but I don't know how."

"He can't see you in the morning?"

"He works."

"Where he work at?"

Miki shrugged. "I didn't ask him."

"What he drive?"

"A truck."

"What kind of truck?"

"An older Silverado."

"But he got a job right?"

"Yeah. He got his own house too. And he has custody of his little girl."

"His own house?"

"I was over there."

"He got a brother, cousin, a friend?"

Miki laughed. "I can ask him."

"Who was that guy he was with that knew Redd?"

"I don't know."

"I've seen him around at other parties but you know Ox be right there so I can't find out nothing," Kat said. She sucked air through her teeth with aggravation. Her phone rang. She answered it. "Hey Mama..."

Miki looked in Redd's direction. He wasn't thinking about her anymore. He was into a game of dominoes.

Kat hung up. "You wanna ride with me over to my mama's?"

"Redd ain't gonna let me go."

Kat grinned and winked her eye. "I got this."

Miki watched Kat skip over to the men. She said something to Ox first then to Redd. She looked back at Miki. Redd glanced back at Miki. Ox gave Kat some money and she came skipping back to Miki. "C'mon girl 'fore he change his mind."

"Where you bitches going?" Toya asked as they dashed inside the house.

"Over my mama's," Kat replied. "We'll be back."

Miki went to get Téa, Chanta, and Montasia. Kat called for her two Nya and OJ.

Kat explained that where her mama was they had a couple of inflatable bouncers for the kids. It was Kat's cousin's little boy's birthday party as well as a Labor Day cookout. Kat's mother wouldn't rest until she brought the kids. That was the only reason Redd gave in. For the kids.

The family gathering was at McArthur Park right next to McArthur Mansion. Miki didn't expect it to be so many people but then again it was the Moores. They always went out for holidays and family gatherings.

The kids got excited when they saw the colorful inflatables.

Kat said, "Look at this shit. This bitch got a fuckin clown."

Miki and the kids followed Kat through the cluster of people.

Random people were speaking to Kat.

Her cousin Shameka called, "Kat! C'mere heifa!"

"Where Kat?" Debra asked looking around.

Nya and OJ said in unison, "Granny!"

Debra spread her arms wide, "C'mere babies!"

"I was wondering when you was gonna show up," Shameka said. She was preparing one of the picnic tables for the kids. "Hey Miki. You mean to tell me Redd let you go somewhere without him?"

Debra looked at Téa, "C'mere girl. You know you my grandbaby too."

Joyce asked, "Debra, who lil girl is that?"

"Kat's friend," Debra said.

“Ain’t she cute,” Teresa said. Teresa was Debra’s sister in law who was also Shameka’s mother. Joyce was Teresa’s first cousin. Miki knew of Teresa but didn’t recognize Joyce.

Debra ushered the kids, “Y’all go play. And be careful!”

Miki turned her attention back to the younger women.

“Kat, you tell Ox where we were going?” Miki asked.

“Yeah. Why?”

Miki looked disappointed. She knew if they stayed gone too long Redd would come looking for her. She couldn’t never enjoy herself anywhere without him.

Deja threw a piece of ice at her brother. “Snap out of it big head!”

Bebe wiped the water from his neck where the ice connected. “Damn Deja. That hurt.”

“You over there daydreaming,” Deja giggled.

“This nigga gone over a bitch,” Julius clowned.

“A girl Bebe?” Deja asked in a teasing tone.

“What girl?” Cyn asked.

Bebe waved them all off dismissively. He looked across the park for Kennedi and BJ. He saw BJ but not Kennedi. Maybe she was with his mother or Bless.

Cyn walked upon him. “You seeing somebody?”

“Whatchu care for?” Bebe asked a bit amused. Cyn was his sister’s best friend who act like she wanted to give up the goods but was only a big tease. Cyn was just how Bebe liked his women. Short, redbone, and thick. She had a cute face too but she reminded him of Stefani. She and Deja stayed in the club. Both were childless and carefree.

"I thought you were waiting on me," Cyn said seductively sticking her chest out placing her hand on her hip.

"I am. Waiting for you to grow up so I can give you this dick." Bebe said playfully.

Cyn rolled her eyes moving away from him, "See...that's what I'm talking about."

"Ay Bebe, you got a lighter?" Pooh asked.

"Naw. I don't smoke," Bebe said. Julius cut the music up in his SUV. A group of young females got excited and started dancing. Bebe knew they were doing a mating dance. Anything to get a man's attention as if the tight ass shorts they had on wasn't enough.

Cyn started swaying her hips from side to side. Her ass was looking good but Bebe had someone else on his mind.

Bebe stay posted up against Julius' SUV enjoying the entertainment. He looked back across the park and saw Bless motioning the kids out of the bouncer. The kids were heading to the sheltered picnic tables. Kennedi got out and looked for her shoes. She looked around and started smiling. She walked over to another little girl and grabbed her hand. They both joined Bless.

Shameka called from the shelter, "Carlos! Y'all come sing happy birthday to my baby!"

"Is she serious?" Pooh asked.

Bebe chuckled, "C'mon man. If it was your child you'd want everybody to participate too."

Julius added, "Yeah nigga, it's for the kids."

"Y'all know how Shameka is," Carlos sighed.

Bebe was held back by Yolanda. "Let me holla at you Bebe."

She pressed up against him. Bebe smiled, "It took you long enough to say something."

"Well you had that lil girl in your face," Yolanda said glancing in Cyn and Deja's direction.

"What's up?" he asked as they began walking.

"You," she said seductively.

"What you want girl?"

"You know what I want."

"I ain't fucking with you like that Yoyo."

"Why not?"

"Cause you don't know what you want." When the words left his mouth Bebe realized he was falling for yet another woman in a similar situation as Yolanda. Like Miki, Yolanda had somebody at home but she couldn't stay away from Bebe. He ended it because he wanted something more. He wanted his own woman. Bebe always ended up with women who couldn't and wouldn't commit.

When Bebe made it to the crowded shelter he noticed the little girl sitting beside Kennedi was the same little girl whose hand she had been holding. The little girl was Téa. He immediately searched for Miki.

Miki already had her eyes on Bebe. When she saw Kennedi, she searched for him. Kennedi called Joyce her "Grandmama" so Miki assumed Joyce was Bebe's mother. She could see the resemblance now.

Miki spotted Bebe before him and the others made it to the shelter. He looked incredibly delicious in his black cap sitting on his head just so and cocked to the side. He wore a square neck black tank with fawn colored shorts that rested on his hips. His bow legs gave him a swag like his dick was too big. Miki screamed on the inside. Remembering Saturday night gave Miki an orgasmic rush throughout her body.

Bebe locked his eyes on her. She was absolutely beautiful. Her twists were piled up on her head in a bun. Her neck appeared slender and delicate. Her narrow shoulders were exposed in the multi-animal print strapless maxi dress. Her breasts sat up full and round. The dress draped over her curves still giving away how shapely she was. How could a waist that small lug around an ass so big?

Everybody sang Happy Birthday except Bebe and Miki. Nothing matter at the moment except wanting to be with each other.

Kat whispered in Miki's ear, "Ain't that him?"

Miki nodded.

"Play it off. There's people here that know Ox and Redd. They will run back and tell."

Miki nodded.

After the singing and cheering Miki coolly followed Kat around the shelter where Bebe was with a group of young adults.

"What's up Kat?" Pooh said. "I didn't know you was here. Where Ox?"

"He at Ronnie's but I don't keep up with that nigga like that," Kat said. "Mama asked me to bring the kids by though."

She looked at Bebe. “Who you kin to?”

“You know Bebe?” Pooh asked.

Deja walked over, “Hey Kat!”

“Hey Deja,” Kat said.

“You know Deja too?” Pooh asked.

“She do my hair,” Deja answered. “And...Let me make sure I get this right. Kat’s mama’s brother is Shameka’s daddy and Shameka’s mama is our mama’s cousin. Did I say it right?”

“So, we share a couple of cousins,” Bebe said to Kat.

Kat asked, “You’re Deja’s brother?”

“Blyss. He’s Bless’ twin,” Deja answered.

Kat was amazed. “Okay, why was I thinking Silas was your only brother?”

Deja laughed. “Kat your mind be on a million things at once.”

Téa came up to Miki, “Mommy, I gotta use it.”

Miki walked off to tend to Téa.

Pooh asked, “Who your friend?”

Before Kat could answer Julius said, “Nigga that’s Redd lady.”

“Who?” Pooh asked.

“Redd, the one that own the shop Kat work at. And he own the club,” Julius said.

“I ain’t never seen him with her,” Pooh said.

Kat said, “That’s because he keep her under lock and key. Give it a few minutes. If I don’t get her back to his ass he’ll be riding through here." She shot Bebe a look.

Bebe got the picture. He wouldn't intentionally cause trouble for Miki. He looked toward the restrooms. How could he talk to her without anyone suspecting anything?

Miki didn't know who the girl was with the coochie cutting capris on and the long Tamar Braxton weave, but Miki wanted her to stop touching on Bebe. It seemed like Bebe was enjoying the attention too. As a matter of fact, she wasn't the only one all over him.

The more she watched Bebe she realized that even if she got with him the idea that he was so popular with the ladies was a threat to Miki's security. He would be just like Redd except he wouldn't hit on her. But then again Miki wasn't sure if Bebe would or wouldn't. She didn't know him that well. Redd didn't show his true colors until eight months down the line.

Kat hurried over to Miki. "I knew it! C'mon, let's go!"

"What?" Miki asked confused by Kat's behavior.

"Them mothafuckas are here!" Kat said. She pulled on Miki. "Get up. Let's go over here by the kids."

Miki heard the loud base of Ox's sound system getting closer.

"Shit."

"What is it?" Shameka asked.

"It's Ox and Redd," Kat said.

Miki and Kat hurried over to where the kids and the older women were sitting. Debra said dryly, "That boy must be here."

"Who?" Joyce asked.

"Her boyfriend," Debra said with a frown. She gestured toward Miki.

Joyce chuckled, "Whatchu move for?"

"So he won't trip," Miki said quietly.

Joyce lowered her voice, "You must gotchu one of them crazy ones."

"Crazy don't even come close," Miki said under her breath.

"You're such a pretty girl. It's a shame you gotta deal with a nut," Joyce tsked. She lowered her voice even more. "You know my son?"

"Who's your son?" Miki asked although she already knew the answer.

"Bebe."

"No, I don't," Miki lied.

Joyce gave Miki a knowing grin. "I know better. I know my son. I know desire in a woman's eyes too."

Miki's mouth dropped open. "What are you saying?"

Joyce chuckled, "I'm saying, y'all know each other or you wanna know each other."

Miki put her finger up to her lips. "Be quiet lady."

Joyce laughed louder. She kept her eyes on the big light skinned guy approaching too. Joyce said, "Your daughter looks just like her daddy."

"I know--Wait! Is he here?" Miki asked in a panicked tone.

"Mmm hmm. So, your daughter and my granddaughter are in the same class?"

"Yeah...how far is he?" Miki asked.

Joyce's eyes traveled over Miki's head. Miki knew Redd was behind her.

"Get the kids and let's go," Redd ordered.

Miki twisted around to look up at Redd. "Hey baby. I didn't know you were coming. When you get here?"

"Bring your ass on," he growled.

Kat said, "Redd I was bringing her back."

"You said thirty minutes."

"But the kids are having a good time. And they had to get some cake," Kat argued.

Redd ignored Kat. He snapped on Miki, "How come the fuck you ain't moving? Getcho mothafuckin ass up!"

Miki realized that just about everybody was silently watching them as she stood to her feet. She was embarrassed as always.

She brushed past him to retrieve the three girls. Téa started to tear up. Her voice came out tiny, "Mama, I don't wanna leave."

"I know baby," Miki said with defeat. "Just come on."

Miki held Téa's and Chanta's hands while Montasia walked behind them. Miki didn't bother looking back. It didn't matter because Redd was right on her. "You got an attitude Miki?"

"No. We getting in Ox's car?"

"Stop walking."

"For what?"

Redd grabbed her by the back of the neck. "Why you wanna keep trying me?"

Téa started crying. Miki pleaded, "I'm not trying you."

He released her pushing her forward at the same time. "Just getcho ass in the car! And shut up Téa!"

Téa clung to Miki's leg. *How can I protect you when I can't protect myself*, Miki thought.

Chapter 7

That was one of the most difficult things Bebe had to sit through. He wanted to intervene so badly, but he knew it would only make matters worse for Miki unless she was ready to walk away from Redd.

It broke his heart to see Téa so miserably upset and obviously scared of her father. When Redd grabbed Miki by her neck Bebe bolted from his seat. He was ready to kick Redd's ass. Pooh, Joyce and Kat stopped him.

Kat said, "Don't. You'll only make things worse for her."

Pooh laughed nervously, "C'mon man Bebe. You can't be fighting everybody's battles. You the only nigga I know who wanna fight every wrong mothafucka in the universe."

"Bebe, sit'cho ass down," Joyce ordered.

Bebe groaned in frustration. "I swear I wanna beat his ass."

Ox walked over to the shelter, "C'mere Kat."

Kat walked away to see what Ox wanted.

Joyce ordered Bebe to sit down right where Miki had been sitting. Bless came over and sat down by Bebe. "What was that?"

Joyce asked Bebe, "How long?"

Bebe kept his eyes on Miki as she got in the car. "How long what Mama?"

Joyce lowered her voice to speak although by now everyone else was talking around them. "You and her?"

Bless put two and two together. She gasped, "Is that her Bebe?"

Bebe's silence answered the question.

"Bebe, you know this won't work," Joyce said. "She gotta get away from that man first."

"She will," Bebe said.

"Then you should wait to pursue something with her," Joyce said. "I know you. You won't be able to sit back for long. And I don't want you creating a bigger problem for yourself."

Bebe removed his hat and rested his face in the palm of his hand propped up on his elbow. He looked at his mother and asked, "How you know every damn thing?"

Joyce smiled, "I just do."

"How you know about...that?" he asked in reference to him and Miki.

"When everybody else was singing happy birthday the two of you were frozen in time just staring at each other. Y'all went out of the way not to speak to each other but neither one of you could take your eyes off the other."

Bless laughed, "You know Mama is a private eye by trade."

Bebe couldn't stop thinking about Miki and wondering if she was okay. He could hardly sleep that night eager for the morning to arrive so he could see her.

Bebe hurried to Kennedi's school as fast as he could. When he got there Téa hadn't been signed in. It was ten "til nine. Bebe waited and she never showed up.

Wednesday came and Bebe waited again. Just when he was about to start his truck's engine he saw her Range pull into the lot. However she wasn't the one driving. Redd was in the driver's seat. Miki and Téa got out and hurried inside the building. Bebe sat back. He needed to see Miki's face.

When Miki exited the building she looked over in Bebe's direction then proceeded to get back in the vehicle with Redd.

Later Bebe sent her a text: *As a reminder we're having a parent meeting tomorrow @ 12. We encourage all parents to participate as these will be held weekly every Thursday. If you will be attending your response will be appreciated.*

Two hours later Miki responded: *I will be there*

Thursday morning Miki saw that Kennedi was already there and signed in. She rushed back outside and called Bebe. He didn't answer but he called her right back. "Miki?"

"Hey. Where are we meeting?"

"At the school. Can you still come?"

"Yeah."

"Okay...I'm happy to hear your voice. Are you alright?"

"I'm okay," she said indifferently.

"Did he hurt you?"

"I'm okay Bebe. I'll see you at twelve."

"Miki, don't do that. Prepare me for what I might see on your body."

"You can't see it."

"Why not?"

"I mean it's not visible." Her other line beeped. It was Redd.

"What do you mean? Did he rape you?"

"That's him calling. I'll see you later." She switched her line over. "Hello?"

"What are you doing?" Redd asked.

"On my way back to the house. I just dropped Téa off."

"I need you back in the house."

"I'm on my way Redd."

"After that meeting shit you get Téa and get your ass back in the house. You hear me?"

"I can still attend the meeting?"

"It's for Téa's school."

"Redd, I don't have nowhere to go anyway. Me and Téa will be home by two."

"Call me when you get to the meeting, when you leave the meeting, and when you and Téa get in the house."

"Okay," She said.

"Miki?"

"What?"

"I love you."

"Love you too," she forced out. Miki ended the call. She exhaled with frustration.

Bebe was at the school right at twelve. Miki pulled up beside him ten minutes later. She was on the phone. She ended the call as she got out of her vehicle. She quickly jumped in on the passenger side of Bebe's truck.

"Were you talking to him?" Bebe asked.

"Yeah," Miki said.

Bebe backed out of his spot. “I don’t appreciate you brushing me off.”

“I wasn’t trying to in a mean way,” Miki said. She looked over at him apologetically. “I’m sorry.”

Bebe looked at Miki. Her expression was somber as if she was on the verge of crying. “Baby, I wasn’t being serious.”

“I know,” she said sadly. She looked out of the passenger window.

“Leave him Miki.”

She didn’t say anything.

Bebe asked, “When you say you can’t see what he done to you, what were you talking about?”

“He hit me in the head. He does that so bruises won’t be visible.”

Bebe had no reply. They didn’t talk the rest of the drive.

When Miki walked in Bebe’s house she asked, “Where’s Shadow?”

“A friend of mine trying to breed. You want anything to eat or drink?”

Miki shook her head. She made her way to his bedroom. They didn’t have much time to waste. Miki removed her clothes and got in bed.

Bebe came into the room and looked at her clothes on the floor. Then he looked at her lying in his bed. “Is this what you wanna do?”

“Yes it is.”

“I need to freshen up. I was working before I went to the school.”

"You're okay baby. Just get in the bed with me."

The soft sweetness of her voice was very soothing. Bebe undressed tossing his clothes beside hers. Miki turned on her side to face him as he got in the bed.

Miki's voice was soft. "Have I told you that I think you're beautiful?"

Bebe blushed. "No."

Miki caressed his face. "Well I'm telling you now. I could look at you all day long." She gave him a soft kiss to the lips. Her hand grazed his body from his neck to his side. Bebe grabbed her hand. Miki smiled as she shook her hand free. She went further and grabbed his hardness and stroked it a few times.

Pushing him on his back Miki straddled him. She took possessive of his mouth with hers kissing him deep and passionate. She kissed his neck and nibbled at his ears. Bebe groaned trying to bear the sensation. Miki was tickled by the fact Bebe was so sensitive.

She kissed lower encircling his nipples with her tongue until they were rigid. She kissed him on his abs and his sensitive sides. He shuddered under her touch whimpering like a baby.

Miki suckled his scrotum and licked the underside of his dick. She did what she did last time, but it wasn't as aggressive.

Bebe watched her as she positioned herself over his dick. Holding him she rubbed his head in between her pussy lips spreading the wetness. She inserted his head inside her. Bebe grabbed her hips to stop her. He said, "Condom."

"I know," she said but completely disregarded him as she lowered herself onto him.

"Miki baby, we need a—"

Miki covered his mouth with hers as she worked her hips. Bebe couldn't resist the feel of her tight wet pussy. It was evident by the way he held onto her driving his dick into her. Miki raised up on her knees and rode him. Bebe reached up and fondled her big D's. Then his hand came down to rub on her clit.

Miki situated herself in a squatting position. She placed her hands on his chest for balance as she began bouncing on his dick. Bebe moaned loudly. "Yes Miki...baby...got-damn..."

Miki spun around with him still inside her and rode him in reverse. Bebe couldn't take her eyes off her ass and how her pussy gripped his dick. She would come down on his dick hard a few times then she would twerk her ass making it wiggle and jiggle up and down.

"Mmm hmm," Bebe moaned. His dick was covered in all her wetness. "Bus' dat pussy open baby."

Miki felt him grope her ass. She guessed he couldn't resist but she felt him ease his thumb in her ass. She wondered if that was a sign he liked anal too. Unable to take it anymore Bebe sat up and slammed his dick into her a few times before forcing her in the doggy style position. Miki cried out with every hard stroke he delivered. She found herself climaxing like last time. She was erupting, and nothing could stop her. She screamed. Bebe groaned. Her whole body shook. Bebe released inside of her.

Miki fell to the bed unable to move. Bebe kissed her back in different spots. Was what he was feeling the same as when people say women put their emotions into sex? Because all Bebe could think about was how he felt like he was falling in love with Miki.

Miki had it bad. So bad that the following Sunday she skipped church and went to Bebe's house. She made sure to ask her sisters to cover for her. Miki took a risk by bringing Téa. She was excited to be with Kennedi. To Miki's surprise, Téa wasn't scared of Shadow. Téa explained she wasn't afraid because her granddaddy had dogs. Téa was an animal lover anyway.

While Téa and Kennedi played in Kennedi's room Bebe was pounding into Miki and dared her to be loud.

Téa wasn't ready to leave when it was time to go. Bebe convinced Miki to let her stay a little longer. He would take Téa to Miki's sister's house as if that was where she was the whole time. Miki was nervous about it but she went along with it. There were no problems.

Miki was able to see Bebe again Tuesday when Redd got caught up with business. After dropping the girls off Miki followed Bebe back to his house. Again, another risky move. This time they managed to spend the whole day together until it was time for Miki to get Téa.

Thursday, they met for their "parent meeting" at twelve.

"Bebe, what do you do that allows you to miss work?" Miki asked. They had already beat each other up in the sheets. Now Miki was sitting at his breakfast bar in the kitchen.

"I mow lawns and put doorknobs on doors," he said casually.

Miki giggled. “Mowing grass and installing doorknobs can’t afford you this house.”

“I’m a drug dealer in disguise. Cutting grass is my coverup.”

“Are you really?”

Bebe chuckled, “Naw girl. I’ve never dealt drugs. Didn’t have to. My parents tried to provide us with a decent upbringing. My daddy owned his own trucking company. My mama used to be a nurse. My second year in the Marines my--”

“W-w-w-wait! You were in the marines?” Miki asked incredulously.

Bebe smiled, “Yeah.”

“Hmm,” Miki pondered. She took a bite of the sandwich he made for her. Redd would never fix her anything to eat.

“As I was saying, my daddy died and left us a nice chunk of change. We sold his business and we got another chunk of change. When I left the Marines I took up horticulture and an apprenticeship in basic construction and I now own my own landscaping and home improvement business. That’s how cutting grass and changing doorknobs afford me this house.”

Miki grinned, “I’m impressed.”

“You are?”

“Yeah, with this sandwich,” Miki joked. “What did you put on it?”

Bebe smiled. “I really like your silly ass.”

“I like yours too.”

Bebe leaned over the counter so that they could peck lips.

"Have you ever worked?" Bebe asked.

"When I was in high school. I met Redd and I haven't worked a day since."

"You were with him in high school?"

"My senior year. I wasn't eighteen yet. It was a struggle just to graduate. He wanted me to quit so I could be available at any time of the day. I had come too far to quit."

"What type of shit is that? The nigga didn't want you finishing high school?"

"Nope. So, going to college was out of the question."

"Do you want to? I mean I know you had aspirations at one point."

Miki gave it some thought. "I did. I used to want to take up theatre and dance. I wanted to be in a Broadway or Off-Broadway play."

"You can still do that."

"He won't let me."

"I'll let you. I'll pay for it."

Miki was thrown. She stared at him blankly.

"Miki, I can make you happy if you give me the chance. But you gotta walk away from Redd."

"Bebe," she sighed. "I really don't want the stress of thinking about making moves...I just wanna enjoy the right now."

"But right now can be forever."

Miki didn't say anything.

Seeing the flustered look on her face Bebe said, "Okay. We

won't get into that, but we will revisit that a later time. I don't want you having any ill feelings toward me."

Miki smiled and decided to change the subject. "I didn't know you can sing?"

"I can't."

"Yes, you can. I heard you singing when Maxwell came on."

"You heard only Maxwell."

"Nope, I heard you," Miki teased. "Sing for me Bebe."

"I can't sing."

Miki got down off her stool and started easing toward Bebe.

Bebe backed up, "Go on Miki."

"Sing for me or else," Miki threatened with a mischievous grin.

"Don't," Bebe begged. Miki chased him around the kitchen center island. He made the mistake by trying to make it to his bedroom. Miki attacked him in the hallway. Bebe fell to the floor in a fit of giggles as Miki tickled him. Miki thought it was so cute for a man to be so ticklish.

As usual when it was time for Miki to leave, they both saddened. Bebe held Miki tight and didn't want to let her go. "When will I see you again? 'Cause I don't think I can go a whole week."

"I was wanting to skip church again, but I think Redd's other kids will be over this weekend. So, I don't know."

Bebe didn't know how long Miki thought they would be able to keep this up. Bebe knew what he felt for her was love, and he loved deeply. Miki was going to have to make a choice; sooner rather than later.

Chapter 8

Bebe had the blues. Not only did he not see Miki Sunday, but she also had to skip their Thursday "meeting". Here it was a whole week later.

When his doorbell rang Friday night Bebe had a good guess who was on the other side of his door. Leaving his rec room Kennedi and Shadow followed him.

"Who that Daddy at the door?" Kennedi asked. Shadow accidentally tripped her.

"Uh-oh," Bebe snickered.

Kennedi bounced back up, "I'm okay."

The doorbell rang again. Bebe swung the door open. BJ knowing the routine stepped inside. Shadow and Kennedi got excited by BJ's presence.

"Can I come in or do you have somebody in there?" Stefani asked.

"Don't you gotta get going? You know, ladies free before ten if you show your pussy?"

"Fuck you," Stefani mumbled. She brushed passed him.

Bebe followed her to his kitchen. She started rummaging through his refrigerator. "I need something on my stomach. Whatchu got in here to eat?"

"I got plenty of go-get-your-own-shit. In a variety of flavors."

"Again...Fuck you," she said rolling her eyes.

The mini dress she wore barely covered her ass. Bebe

asked, “When are you going to stop this?”

“Stop what?”

“All this clubbing shit. Being nonchalant about life. Grow up.”

Stefani stood upright and looked at Bebe, “Honestly, I’m giving myself ‘til the first of the year. Come January first I’ma be a new me.”

“That’s in four months.”

Stefani half-shrugged. “Okay. I have four months to get all this shit out of my system.”

“How old are you?”

“Twenty-seven. Why do you care about all that anyway?”

“You’re my son’s mother. I should care.”

Stefani sniffed the air. “I smell pizza.”

“It’s down in the rec room.”

“And you weren’t going to tell me?”

Bebe watched Stefani’s ass the whole time they walked to the rec room. Stefani was very sexy. She was short, about five feet two inches tall. She had a tight body like a dancer. She was mixed with Puerto Rican and she wore her black hair straightened which fell to the small of her back.

Bebe still cared for Stefani. If she got herself together like she described in the lie she just told, Bebe would consider her again as a woman he would want to marry. Although her immature behavior got on his nerves sometimes she and Bebe still had a good friendship. They even fooled around. Before Miki, she was the last person he had slept with.

The kids along with Shadow played off to the side. Bebe

sat beside Stefani on the couch where she helped herself to his pizza.

"Bebe, why you home on a Friday night anyway?" she asked.

"Uhm...so that I can be here when your stankin' ass come by to drop my son off," he said sarcastically.

"Whatever. If you weren't here I coulda—"

"I don't wanna hear that. You would have blown my phone up asking me where I was."

Stefani grinned, "You right."

"I know I'm right. But you know I gotta work in the morning."

"Who's gonna watch the kids?"

"Deja."

"What are your plans for tomorrow?"

"I don't know. Keonte want me to come out to a bike party. I might bring out my baby. I hadn't rode my bike in a while."

"I wanna ride. Can I go with you?" she asked. She added with seduction, "Bebe you know I like to ride."

Bebe smiled, "I know you do."

Stefani turned to face him, tucking one leg under her and the other leg hung over the couch. She gave Bebe a perfect view of her pink panty covered love box. She said, "How about I skip the club tonight and chill here with you and the kids instead?"

His dick was already pulsating with life. Bebe reached out and touched her through her panties. "Can I get some of this?"

"What do you think?"

Bebe lowered his voice, "I think I need to see how your pussy feel about it." He hooked his finger around the crotch of her panties and inserted it inside her.

Stefani moaned, "Mmm...How do she feel about it?"

Bebe leaned over and kissed her. "She feel good about it."

The next morning Bebe was so worked over he got off to a late start. He had to admit though, waking up to Stefani in his bed and the kids and Shadow coming in the room felt good. It was what Bebe wanted. A completed family of his own. His own woman.

Miki found herself feeling more and emptier. Bebe got her thinking about what she wanted for herself. She used to envision herself as a smart happy well-rounded and grounded successful independent woman. Over time she lost her vision when she got used to not thinking for herself.

It was time Miki reevaluated her life. If not, she knew time would fly by and she would have spent it unhappy. Come January she would be enrolled and registered in somebody's school. Hopefully she would be away from Redd too.

She wanted to leave him. She could walk away and find her own place. But he'd find her, drag her back home and damn near kill her. He had done so several times in the past when she left.

If she left this time could Bebe protect her? Could she trust him to be there for her? She hated dragging him into her mess, but she didn't have any other males in her life willing to stick their neck out for her. Most men stepped back and didn't want to get involved. People would say, she have to want change for herself. Miki did want it but it wasn't as easy for her as people wrote it off to be. She feared Redd. She felt powerless, hopeless, helpless, and lost.

"Miki, you doing it again. What's wrong with you?"

"Oh nothing. I was just thinking about going to school."

Redd cut his eyes at her. "Haven't we discussed this before?"

"Yeah about five years ago."

"And I still feel the same way I did five years ago. You don't need school baby. You got me."

"What if something happens to you? I need something to fall back on."

"If something happens to me you and the kids will still be taken care of."

"Maybe the kids but not me. I'm not your wife."

Redd grinned knowingly.

"Raquel will get everything. I'm just a baby mama."

"If that's what you think," Redd chuckled.

Miki cut her eyes at him as he drove. Why was that funny? He can giggle all he wanted but Miki was determined to go to school.

Ace of Spades Bike Club was having a party at The Cut. Miki was actually surprised Redd told her she was going. Just like last time there were custom painted and tricked out bikes outside of the club. Inside the club people were everywhere representing their bike clubs.

Redd escorted Miki to a particular section where she was

united with Kat and Mokeba. "Hey ladies."

"Hey! Let me get those shoes," Mokeba called out.

Miki sat down looking at her spiked cheetah print and black leather, red-heeled Louboutins. "Girl, these things are old."

"They Louboutins girl. They can't get old," Mokeba said.

Kat straightened Miki's hair. "Your hair makes me jealous."

"I'm just now noticing your twists are out," Mokeba said.

Miki smooth her hair with her hand. Kat had just done it earlier that morning. Miki's hair was styled in an asymmetric bob with an off-centered part. The right fell into her eye and the longest section touched her clavicle. The left reached her shoulder and the back rested at the base of her neck. With all of the body in it and how black it was people assumed it was weave but it was hers. Having a best friend as a hairdresser had its privileges.

Kat continued to mess with Miki's hair while whispering, "Your man is here."

Miki knew who Kat was talking about. She needed to see him. She missed him so much. It had been a week since being with Bebe. Even if she was on her period that whole week just to be in his presence would have been satisfying. They saw each other Thursday morning when Miki arrived early just to tell him she wouldn't be able to make it to the meeting. He seemed upset, but he said he was okay.

Miki whispered, "Where is he?"

"He was by the bar. He looking good too along with that cousin of his."

Miki scanned the perimeter first. No Bebe by any of the bars. She searched the dancefloor. There he was dressed in all white. Kat was right, Bebe looked damn good. He was having a good time grinding on the girl he was with. Pocahontas was working her ass on him too. Miki felt a little jealous, but she was probably just some random girl.

Miki's smile faded when she witnessed Bebe hold the girl from behind and kiss her. He said something in her ear. Pocahontas turned around and playfully hit him. She took his hand and led him off the floor.

Miki didn't care if Redd got mad, but she had to get closer.

"Where you going?" Kat asked.

"I'll be back," Miki said absently.

"Miki! You know how Redd is."

Miki stepped down to the dance floor and walked around the perimeter. She ignored the stares and advances. She stopped in front of the bar because she had a perfect view of Bebe and the cluster of people he was with.

Bebe and Pocahontas were very familiar with each other. Very friendly and very close. He still held onto her and she held on to him. They looked like a happy couple. Miki didn't know what to think. She was disappointed. So when he wasn't with her, Bebe was with other women. Miki couldn't trust him anymore nor believe he would be all those things he talked about being for her.

Chapter 9

Bebe's mind was far from being on Miki. Was he intentionally pushing her out of his mind? Yes. As much as he wanted to believe she would leave Redd the reality was Miki wasn't going no time soon.

Bebe couldn't be with Miki whenever he wanted. He couldn't take her out. He couldn't show her off as his lady. His mother was right. His patience was shorter than it used to be.

Stefani said, "Bebe buy me a drink."

"You need to slow down," Bebe laughed. "Remember we rode in on my bike. If your ass can't hold on BJ won't have a mama no more."

"Shut up silly," Stefani said. "I've only had two drinks."

"C'mon with your spoiled ass," Bebe said pulling her by the hand.

Heading towards the bar hips and ass gloved in white straight jeans caught Bebe's eye. The platform pumps the girl had on were sexy. Bebe glanced at her face and realized she was looking right in his face wearing a very devastated expression.

Bebe's heart jumped out of his chest and smacked the shit out of him. It was Miki. Her hair was different. But her amber eyes that he loved looking into were filled with sadness.

Bebe turned away from her and continued to the bar with Stefani. She said, "I loved her shoes. I bet if I wasn't with you you'd holla at her, wouldn't you?"

Bebe looked back. Miki was still standing there but she

had turned around to continue to stare at him. Where was Redd? Wasn't she afraid of people knowing about them? He didn't know what she wanted him to do.

Miki was hurt but what could she do. When Bebe turned his back to her she turned away with her shoulders dropped and walked to the restroom. She went in one of the stalls and leaned up against the door. Bebe was with another woman. And Redd was going to beat her ass. She didn't even care anymore. The enthusiasm she felt at first for making a change in her life and leaving Redd suddenly disappeared.

"Miki."

What the hell? "Why are you in the women's restroom?"

"Fuck that shit. Open the door," Bebe said.

"I'm using it. Leave me alone."

"So, you got a dick now? Cause your feet are facing the toilet."

A girl came into the restroom and gasped at the sight of Bebe. He said, "I'm talking to somebody, but you can handle your business."

The girl said, "Uhm...I'll just go to another one." She left.

Miki opened the door. "You need to get out."

"I wanna talk to you," Bebe said. He grabbed her wrists to pull her to him.

Miki resisted and pulled away. "No Bebe."

Bebe wrapped his arms around her anyway. "Baby please."

"Bebe you got somebody out there. And I got somebody too."

"She's my son's mama."

"You still fuck your son's mama?"

Bebe flipped it on her. "You still fuck your daughter's daddy?"

Miki tried to push him away. "You know my situation. I don't have sex with Redd because I want to."

"But the mothafucka still get to dig in my pussy."

"Your pussy?" Miki asked taken aback.

"Yes, it's mine," Bebe smirked. He pressed into her body and gripped her ass with both hands. "Miki, I want you so bad."

Miki wrapped her arms around his neck as they shared a deep passionate kiss.

Bebe whispered, "I wanna fuck you. Can I have you right here?"

"No, we'll get caught," Miki whispered.

Bebe pulled her into the furthest stall. "Take your shoes off and put them on the back of the toilet."

Miki looked at him with confusion.

Bebe undid his pants. "Just do it. Pull your pants down and get up on the toilet."

Miki didn't understand why she wasn't terrified. She was actually excited. The thought of Redd catching her was far from her mind. With her ass tooted in the air Bebe fucked her in the bathroom stall of a club. Miki had never done such a thing. Not even with Redd.

Kat had one eye on the restroom and one eye on Redd. Redd hadn't notice Miki wasn't there yet. Come on Miki, Kat thought. She watched Miki the entire time. She saw Miki staring at Bebe with the other girl. She saw Bebe recognize Miki and ignore her. She watched Miki go to the restroom. Then Bebe said something to the girl. He left, and his retarded ass went into the ladies restroom. That was fifteen minutes ago.

"Kat, where is Miki?" Redd asked looking around.

"Uh...she went to the bathroom. She said her stomach hurt. I'll go check on her," Kat said walking away before Redd could say anything else.

Kat went to the restroom. She heard low moaning sounds. She looked under all the stalls. The last one at the far end. She couldn't see Miki's feet, but she could see a man's feet. No, they are not fucking in the restroom in the club! Kat snickered to herself. She said carefully, "Y'all hurry up. Redd is looking for you Miki."

They act like they didn't hear Kat because Miki got louder and Bebe's breathing quickened. The bathroom door open. Two women wanted to come in. Kat turned them away, "This bathroom is out of order. It flooded."

Miki heard Kat loud and clear. As soon as Bebe finished she got down. They both straightened their clothes. She slipped her shoes back on.

Miki looked at Kat innocently. Kat was grinning. "Y'all two are the boldest mothafuckas I know."

Miki asked, "Where's Redd?"

"Probably on his way over here. So, Miki, me and you should go out first. Bebe wait a few seconds and go in the men's restroom."

Bebe grabbed Miki pulling her to him. He kissed her

softly. He looked into her eyes and whispered against her lips, "I love you."

Miki was stunned as she pulled away. She looked back at him before she exited the bathroom with Kat.

Bebe leaned on the wall length vanity and looked in the mirror at himself. He didn't know that guy staring back at him. He was a confused person. Right when he convinced himself that he didn't want to deal with Miki's situation, as soon as he see her, all of that goes out of the window. He never felt this way about a woman so soon. And what was that "I love you" shit? It just came out. But it was what he felt. Fuck! Bebe passionately wanted Miki. He wouldn't walk away just yet.

Miki pretended to be sick, so Redd wouldn't want sex when they got home. "Baby, something got my stomach messed up."

"I bet it does," Redd said without care. He was distracted by going through Miki's phone.

Miki wasn't worried about the phone. Nothing in it would get her in trouble. She had been very careful with that. "I'm getting in the shower."

"What for?"

"I had a bowel movement earlier. I don't feel clean and my butt itch," she said casually going into the bathroom. She wrapped her hair and tied it down with a silk scarf. She eased her blouse over her head and slipped out of her pants and panties. She hurried to dispose of her clothes. She put them deep in the dirty clothes hamper. Removing her bra and slipping on her shower cap Miki stepped inside the walk-in shower. She immediately started washing up.

Five minutes into her shower the door opened. Next thing she knew she was being yanked out. Redd delivered two punches to her back as she fell to the floor. "Who the fuck is he?"

"Who?" Miki cried. She looked up at him.

"The nigga you fucking?"

"I'm not fucking nobody—No Redd!" she screamed as he hit her again.

"Bitch stop motha—" he paused to deliver two blows to the top of her head, "...fuckin lying!"

Miki tried to back away while still trying to shield herself. She cried and pleaded, "Please baby...I'm not...please."

He started punching on her from every direction as he cussed her out in between blows. He stopped long enough to turn the shower off. He grabbed the wet washcloth she was using and whipped her once with it. "You ain't about to make a mothafuckin fool outta me. Bitch, I will kill you and him!"

"I ain't seeing nobody Redd. I promise," she cried. The sting of the washcloth could still be felt.

"Listen, you dumb ass hoe. My boy Tommy told me he saw you with some nigga at the club. You and Kat think y'all real mothafuckin slick."

"Baby when I go on the floor a lot of dudes be in my face," Miki tried to reason.

"Why the fuck you hide your clothes? Huh?" He kicked her thigh. "Why the fuck you hiding your clothes!" He kicked her again, this time more forcefully.

Miki cried holding out her hands in a surrendering way. "Baby please...I promise..."

"Miki, I dug your clothes out. They smell like a man's cologne. Not mine. And your panties were wet. You let the nigga play in your pussy?"

"No," Miki cried.

"Get up!"

Miki's head was throbbing, and her body already ached. She tried to push up off the floor. Redd kicked her right back down.

"I said get up."

Miki tried again but he kicked her down again.

"You need to tell me who this nigga is." Redd said.

"I can't tell you because it ain't nobody..." Miki breathed.

"I got all night. You won't leave this goddamn house. You ain't getting your phone back either."

Miki started sobbing.

"Shut the fuck up!" he spat. "Now getcho ass up!"

Miki used the cabinets to pull up on.

"Get in the bed," he ordered.

"I'm wet," Miki said.

"Get in goddamn bed like I said!"

Miki took her cap off and tossed it aside. She went to the bed and got in. Redd commenced to violently violate her. He was actually raping her because Miki was not consenting. It was rough and brutal. He even took anal from her.

Miki had to stay in bed even the next day. Redd would have his way with her all day. Redd told everybody that called her phone that Miki wasn't feeling too good.

He was sitting in the bed with her watching television when Miki's phone rang again. Redd picked it up and looked at it. He said, "Ms. Brenda calling."

Miki grew nervous. She was ready to run if Redd answered her phone.

He accepted the call. "Hello?"

Miki tried to ease out of bed. Redd said, "Uh-uh where you going? Lay back down...Hello?"

Miki laid back down and watched Redd ready to block his blows.

Redd said, "She don't feel too good...Her stomach...Uh-huh, that's probably it...She should be better by Thursday, but that'll be up to her if she feel like making it...Nah, she ain't been wanting to talk to anybody...I'll tell her...I will. You too...Bye."

Redd turned to Miki, "You know for a minute I didn't think Ms. Brenda was a real person. I was beginning to think that was your dude and y'all text in code."

Miki don't know what Bebe did or who Redd was talking to but Miki was relieved. She could hear Bebe in her head disguising his voice to sound like a woman. He was just that silly. Miki laughed out loud.

"What's funny?" Redd asked.

"You. I'ma have to tell Ms. Brenda what you said," Miki said.

Redd said, "That's what I thought for real."

Thursday needed to get there fast.

"Your ass is retarded," Deja giggled.

Joyce shook head in shame. "He ain't got a bit of sense."

Bebe chuckled, "Did I sound convincing?"

"He bought it," Joyce said.

Bebe's smile faded. "I can't stand his ass. I know he done jumped on her. He got her phone and I heard him telling her to lay back down. I wanna kick his ass."

"Bebe, what did I say?" Joyce said.

"I know Mama, but I can't walk away from Miki like that." He slumped lower on the sofa in his mother's den.

"She got you whipped," Deja teased.

Dinky said, "Hell yeah this nigga whipped. He can't even work a whole day anymore."

"Call me whatever you want. I'm getting Miki away from him. Her and Téa," Bebe said factually. He lowered his cap over his eyes.

"Well what's up with you and Stefani?" Deja asked.

"Nothing," Bebe said. "You know that girl buck."

"But y'all seemed real cozy yesterday," Deja said.

Bebe didn't want to talk about Stefani. His mind was on Miki.

When Bebe came out of the restroom and back out to the floor Miki was talking to Redd. She sat down. Five minutes later some guy whispered something in Redd's ear. Bebe could see the difference in Redd's demeanor. He went back to Miki and made her leave with him.

Miki didn't text him like she does when she attend church.

He knew she couldn't still be mad at him. Something just didn't seem right. Bebe felt it. That's why he had to call. He wanted to hear her voice but instead he got Redd's.

Bebe's phone started ringing. He answered it without looking at it, "Yeah"

"Bebe," the voice whispered.

"What? Why you sound like that?"

"Can you please come over here?" Bless said.

Bebe sat up. He could hear the panic in his sister's voice. "What's wrong?"

"One of the boys let Marvin in."

"What's he doing?"

"Nothing yet. I just want him out of my place before he start anything."

"I'm on my way," Bebe said standing abruptly.

"What's wrong?" Joyce asked.

"Marvin at Bless' house. C'mon Dinky, ride with me." Bebe said.

When Bebe got to his sister's house Marvin had Bless cornered in in the kitchen.

"What's up?" Bebe asked.

Bless looked relieved when she saw Bebe and Dinky. Marvin turned around and looked at Bebe and scoffed. "Whatchu over here for? Ain't nobody doing anything to your sister. You called him Bless?"

"I'm over here 'cause this is my sister's house. Don't worry about if she called me or not. I'm here nigga," Bebe said nastily.

Marvin raised his hands in peace. "Chill. I'm just over here to see my boys and see how my wife doing. That's all."

"She a'ight. And your boys are in the living room where you need to be," Bebe said without hesitation. He took a seat at the kitchen table. "Bless, why you didn't come over Mama's? You know she cooked."

Bless glanced at Marvin before she answered, "I was on my way."

"This mothafucka stopped you?" Bebe asked gesturing towards Marvin.

"I didn't stop her from doing anything," Marvin chuckled. "I ain't put no gun up to her head."

"Did you ask him to leave?" Bebe asked.

Marvin answered, "No. She wanted me over here."

"Bitch! I didn't ask you shit," Bebe snapped. "I asked my sister a question."

Marvin started ranting, "See Bless, this was one of our biggest problems. Your damn family always wanna interfere in our business."

"If my sister call me and she need me then her business is my business," Bebe countered. He looked at Bless and asked, "Are you ready for him to leave?"

Marvin looked at Bless. "You don't want me here?"

Bless avoided eye contact with Marvin. He was trying to intimidate her with his stare. Bebe didn't wait for Bless to say anything. He knew his sister, and she was too sweet. Bless didn't want Marvin there. Bebe said calmly, "Get out."

Marvin continued to stare at Bless, “You ain’t gon’ say nothing?”

“She ain’t got to,” Bebe said. “Say bye to your sons and get gone.”

Marvin spun around and spat, “You know I’m tired of your mothafuckin mouth! You always wanna--”

Bebe sprang from his seat before Dinky could grab him. Bebe managed to punch Marvin once before Bless got in the way. “Who the fuck you talking to!”

“No Bebe,” Bless pleaded.

Dinky grabbed Bebe, “C’mon man Bebe.” He looked at Marvin, “Dude, you need to get on.”

Marvin was holding the side of his face. He let out a nervous chuckle, “That’s assault Bebe.”

“Whatchu gon’ do? Call the mothafuckin police? Go ‘head!” Bebe dared.

Marvin looked at Bless, “I’ll talk to you later...Check your brother.”

“Just go,” Bless mumbled.

Lil Marvin and Marcus were watching. As Marvin walked by them, he didn’t even tell them bye. Marvin was there for one reason only. To put fear in Bless. Bebe wasn’t having it, especially since Bless was taking the necessary steps to get away from Marvin.

Bebe said, “Get you and the boys some stuff. Y’all staying at my house for a few days. I don’t trust him.”

Bless gathered some items and did just that.

Chapter 10

Redd took Téa to school Monday and Tuesday. By Wednesday he allowed Miki to take her to school. Miki tried to get there as early as she could to run into Bebe. She had gotten there too early. After dropping Téa off in her classroom Miki strolled down the corridor expecting to see Bebe come in through one of the double doors at the end. He never walked through. She got to her vehicle, started the engine and reached for her seatbelt. She looked out of the front window and could see Bebe hurrying Kennedi inside the building.

Miki thought about blocking his truck so that he would see her, but it seemed as if he was in a hurry. She gave it a few minutes and called his cellphone. No answer. She called it again.

"Hello?" a female voice answered.

Miki was thrown. "I think I dialed the wrong number."

The female said, "That's okay." And ended the call.

Miki looked down at her phone to make sure she had dialed Bebe's number. Plain as day it said Ms. Brenda. Did he get his number changed?

Bebe came flying out of the building and half ran half walked to his truck. He was in a hurry. Miki didn't bother him. She felt dispirited as she watched him pull off in his truck.

Miki went home and thought about the woman who answered Bebe's phone. She wondered who that could have been. Maybe it was Pocahontas. It saddened Miki to realize that Bebe may need to just move on if he was looking for happiness. She wasn't sure if she had what it took to leave Redd.

After about thirty minutes of being home she got a text notification.

Ms. Brenda: you call?

Miki: Are you able to talk?

Ms. Brenda: yeah

Miki dialed his number. He answered on the first ring. "Hey."

"Hey."

"Are you okay?" he asked with concern.

"Yeah, I'm fine."

"How bad did he hurt you?"

"It ain't nothing," she lied.

"It is something. Why did he do it? Did somebody tell him about us?"

"Yeah. Somebody told him they saw me with a man at the club. Then I tried to hide my clothes and he dug 'em out to smell on 'em and shit."

"Baby, I'm sorry 'cause that was my fault."

"You straight. Regardless if it was you or not, it would have happened for another reason anyway."

"Can I see you today?"

"It's not a good idea. He'll probably call or come home around lunchtime."

"You know what? I wouldn't put it past his ass if he had

some type of device recording your conversation or something hidden somewhere."

Then the thought occurred to Miki that the surveillance cameras could easily tell on her. Shit! She just hoped Redd didn't get the same idea and think of the cameras. "You're right. But I was just calling to let you know I'm fine. I'll see you Friday."

"Friday?"

"He's going out of town Friday. I told him I didn't feel like going out of town with him. But I think he has his own agenda for not wanting me to go with him anyway."

"So that's why you said Friday and not tomorrow?"

"I figure we could just wait unless you wanna still meet tomorrow."

"Hell yeah, I wanna see you. I need to see you."

Miki smiled. "Okay. I'll see you tomorrow then."

"Bye Miki. I love you."

Miki ended the call. She wasn't sure if she should have asked him about the woman that answered his phone earlier. It wasn't really her place to question him but she still wanted to know. She decided she would wait and ask tomorrow.

The following day just as Miki was about to leave for her Thursday parent meeting Redd showed up at the house.

"Ay baby," Redd said from the bedroom. "Skip that thing today."

"Why is that?" she asked. Her keys were already in her hand and she was headed to the door.

"Because I said so," he said. He appeared at the end of the

hall. He looked at Miki with lust in his eyes. "C'mere."

"What Redd?" Miki asked with a bit of annoyance.

"Don't what me. Just c'mere."

Miki walked over to where he was. He pecked her forehead and pulled her close into a warm hug. "I want us to start doing better."

"What do you mean?" she asked.

"You know. Us and how we get along. We gotta stop all this bullshit arguing."

Ain't this some shit? He never accepted sole blame. He somehow had to always make it seem as if Miki was just as guilty. Miki knew better. She just wouldn't vocalize her opinion. However, she said, "Well my biggest issue with you is your cheating and when you...hit me."

"I don't fuck around. You think I got time to mess around?" he asked innocently.

"I know you mess around. Alicia and Tamika be dropping little slick shit."

"Fuck them. They just jealous of you and wanna be where you are and shit. Fuck them," he barked. He took Miki by the hand and led her to their bedroom. "Take them clothes off."

Shit. The only thing Miki could hope for was that Bebe didn't call or text her phone to raise suspicion.

Redd started kissing on her neck and behind her ears. Miki began to disassociate herself. Sex with Redd had become redundant. She knew exactly what he would do, what positions he would put her in, and what he would request of her. He would lick her pussy then he would shove his dick in her face as if that's what they agreed on. She didn't want to suck his dick. He went around putting it in too many people. But if she objected it would be a problem. So, she half-heartedly sucked it.

He got on top of her and pumped in and out. She wasn't wet enough. He let spit fall from his mouth down to his dick that was still inside Miki. She hated that too. She thought, *if I'm not wet then that means I don't wanna do it with you dummy*!

It seemed as if he couldn't bust a nut. Miki was becoming drier. He reached over to the nightstand to get the lubricant out of the top drawer. Miki should have been happy to see the bottle, but she wasn't. Just as she thought, after lubing up he let some drizzle on her rectum. She looked up at him, "I don't wanna do that."

"Just a lil bit," he said. He began short stroking his way inside her ass.

Miki was supposed to relax but it was the worse feeling ever. She wanted him to stop.

"Relax," he whispered.

Miki remembered to breathe as she tried to relax. She figured the sooner he get a good rhythm the sooner it will be over with. It seemed like it took him forever. She thanked the Almighty when he was done.

She looked at the time. It was only 12:10. She could still get an hour in with Bebe.

"What you looking at the time for?" Redd asked. He was lying on his back watching her.

"Tryna see if I could still make it to the meeting. I think they were going to discuss a bakeoff for the kids today," she lied. She didn't know where these lies came from. Now she could see how easy it was for lies to drip from Redd's tongue.

"They'll catch you up next week," he said.

Miki didn't want to be in the house with him. She couldn't wait until it was time to get Téa.

Bebe was agitated. He wanted to call Miki and just call off the entire relationship. He couldn't keep doing this playing some side piece for Miki. She was going to have to make a decision. It was either him or Redd. If she chose Redd, then that would be on her. He couldn't play savior for everybody. His mother and Dinky both fussed at him about it. But if Bebe was honest there was something about Miki that he wanted to save.

He was so mad he wasn't sure if he even wanted to see her Friday, but she said she would be over as soon as she parked her car at her sister's house. Who wanted to go through these changes just for some ass? Sometimes he felt like he would be better off trying to make something work with Stefani's wild self. At least with her he could have her as often as he wanted. He could go out in public with her. Go on dates like normal couples do.

The doorbell rang. Expecting it to be Miki he didn't bother asking who it was before opening the door. It was Deja and Cyn. They were dressed and ready for somebody's club.

"What's up, bruh?" Deja said as she walked inside his house.

Cyn smiled up at him making sure to throw her breasts up at him. "Hey Bebe."

"Why are y'all at my house?" he asked as he closed the door behind them.

"Just stopping by. You got something to eat?" Deja asked immediately going to his kitchen.

Cyn asked, "What's up with you Bebe?"

"Nothing," he mumbled.

Cyn looked him up and down like she wanted to eat him. He chuckled, "What is your problem?"

"Why you say that?" she grinned.

"Why you looking at me like that?"

"Cause every time I see you it seem like you get sexier. I don't know Bebe. We might have to stop playing games."

"Who's playing games? I don't play them; you the one bullshittin'," he said.

"Whatever," she rolled her eyes.

"Well c'mon then. Tell my sister you'll holla at her later and let's go to my room."

Cyn called out, "Deja! I'll see you in a minute."

"Where you going?" Deja asked.

Cyn looked back up at Bebe from under her lashes. She tried to wear an innocent seductive expression. Bebe walked upon her thinking how cute she was and how many ways he could fuck her. He said, "You ain't ready."

Frustrated Cyn said, "Yes I am. You always do me like that."

"Cause you're my sister's friend. Y'all will fall out once you fall in love with this dick girl. You ain't ready," he boasted.

"Whatever Bebe. You just scared you might fall in love with this pussy. Now," she challenged.

"Well let me see," he said grabbing her hand. He started leading her to his bedroom. Cyn didn't object. Thinking of Miki and just because he could toy with Cyn he let her hand go and said, "I'm just playing. Girl go on!"

"Ooh! You make me sick," Cyn exclaimed. She started playfully hitting on him. "You always playing with my emotions Bebe."

"I love you though," Bebe teased. He decided to give her a hug just as Miki let herself in the front door. He and Cyn both looked over at Miki who was staring back at them. Bebe immediately released Cyn from his hold. "Hey baby."

Miki asked, "Am I interrupting?"

"No. We were just playing around," Bebe explained.

Deja stepped into the great room to be nosey. She recognized Miki as Kat's friend, the one that had been at the park on Labor Day. So that's who he's been talking about all this time.

Miki looked over at Cyn and cut her eyes back to Bebe. She said, "I'll come back once your company has left."

"You ain't gotta do that. It's just my sister and her friend," he said walking towards her.

"Whatever," Miki murmured and went back out of the door.

Bebe shook his head and glanced at Cyn. She was wearing a sneaky grin. He asked, "What's so funny?"

"Your girlfriend mad," Cyn said.

Bebe blew out air in exasperation. He went after Miki. She was walking fast so he had to jog to catch up with her. "Miki stop."

"I don't know what I'm thinking," she said to no one in particular as she kept walking.

"What are you talking about?" he asked keeping beside her.

"Me and you. Why am I even doing this? I keep getting my ass beat, I can't be with you like I want, and I know you won't wait around for much longer," she said as tears filled her lids.

"All you have to do is leave him. You can stay with me."

"I can't," she cried. "He will find me, and he will kill me. I know he will."

"Not as long as I'm around...Will you slow down?"

Miki stopped. She looked up at Bebe as tears streamed down her face. "I feel so stuck Bebe and don't nobody understand me. It's so easy for y'all to say leave him but I can't."

"Who is y'all?"

"You! My sisters, my mama...Kat..."

"Well we can't all be wrong in telling you to do so. All you gotta do is walk away. I'll protect you and we can get the police involved."

"I can't call the police on him," Miki said as she started walking again.

Bebe grabbed her by her arm and spun her around back in the direction of his house. "Let's go to my house and talk about this."

Miki turned around to go to her sister's house. "I think I just need to go to my sister's house and think some stuff out."

Bebe spun her around again. "You can do that at my house. We can come up with something together."

Miki shook her head. "You need to move on. I'll never be able to be anything more for you."

Bebe stopped her from moving by grabbing either of her arms. "Listen. I'm not letting you go to your sister house right now. You're coming back with me and I'm not taking no for an answer. So stop this shit."

Miki averted her gaze from him. She looked anywhere but his face. "You like your sister's friend?"

"There's nothing between me and Cyn. She just come around with my sister and get on my nerves. That's all."

Miki thought about what it would take to leave Redd. It would be hell. She didn't want to have to send him back to prison but Redd would get things to that point. He had an invincible attitude and thought nothing, or nobody could stop him from wreaking havoc. She asked Bebe, "Why do you want me so much?"

"I don't know...," he shrugged. He took her hands in his. "It's just something about you. You're beautiful as hell. You have a softness about you I can appreciate. I know I can bring out the best in you. I feel passionate about seeing you fulfill your own dreams. You need a man that will love you Miki. I'm that nigga."

Miki smiled big. "You are?"

"I'm the one. It don't get no better than me," he bragged proudly.

Miki laughed. "You're so full of yourself."

He kissed her forehead softly. When he pulled back they stared into each other's eyes expressing a desire for the other. Then their lips met in a soft sensual kiss. It awakened Miki's inner being as it always did when she was with Bebe. She needed him. She just had to get to a point where she could trust that he would protect her.

Chapter 11

Miki flopped down on Kat's couch. Her emotions caught up in her dilemma. However, she had pushed her issues aside to be there for Kat.

Kat slowly walked to her kitchen. "If you were pregnant," Kat started. She got distracted by what was in the refrigerator. She continued, "Would you tell Bebe?"

"Nope. Bebe would want me to keep the baby. I know he would."

"How you know? You act like y'all been together forever and you know that man like that," Kat teased.

"It's been a little over a month, but I swear it feels like it's been years."

Kat smiled. She wished her friend would wake up and smell the coffee. Bebe was a good dude. Miki's fear was preventing her from experiencing a true love that would surely make her happy. But then again, Kat was faced with the same issue. "I can tell he's really feeling you?"

"The feeling is definitely mutual."

"So, you wouldn't tell him for real?"

Miki shook her head.

"I wish you could be with Bebe. Just like I wished I could be with a certain person."

"Who? I know you ain't talking about Ox."

"Naw. Fuck him," she said. She smiled as thoughts of Dwayne entered her mind. "He ain't nothing like Ox."

"Are you sure you like him then?" Miki joked.

"Yeah. I mean he's kinda like him but he don't sell drugs or nothing. He got a legit job."

"Is it the doctor dude? Did you get that man's number?"

Kat laughed. "Naw girl. I should have. How 'bout I gotta go see him again."

"Get his number next time."

"So, he can look at me like I'm crazy," Kat said. "He probably don't date females like me. I want a nigga like Bebe anyway."

Miki thought about the night before and the memories made her shudder, her stomach quivered, and her pussy ached. Bebe knew he was the shit in the sheets. She couldn't get enough. She hated the fact that she had to leave when she did. She could have stayed in Bebe's bed for the whole day, but she knew Redd was coming home.

Miki's phone rang. She rolled her eyes. She answered. "Hello?"

"Where are you?" It was Redd. He sounded perturbed.

"I'm at Kat's."

"Oh, so your hot ass didn't go to church. Where's Téa?" His attitude was nasty.

"She's with Maddie," she answered. Her heart began to pound as nervousness consumed her. Téa was not with Maddie. Miki had actually left Téa at Bebe's to play with Kennedi.

"Go get Téa and bring your ass home."

"Ok—"

"Now!"

Miki looked at her phone as it flashed that the call had ended. She looked at Kat and rolled her eyes with aggravation. "That's his ass. He want me to come home. I guess that means he's here."

Kat looked disappointed. "That means Ox on his way too."

Miki got up grabbing her purse and keys. "Well I guess I talk with you later."

"You make sure you call me."

Miki hurried back over to Bebe's. When Bebe answered the door, Miki didn't bother stepping inside. "Where's Téa? We gotta go."

"What's the problem?" Bebe asked.

"Redd's home and he wanna see us," Miki said. Her phone started ringing again. She retrieved it from her purse. It was Redd. She hit ignore to send him to voicemail. She figured she would deal with that when she got home.

Bebe disappeared. Seconds later a sad Téa was coming out of the door. "Mommy, I wanna stay here."

Kennedi was standing beside Bebe. "Why ain't she can stay?"

Miki chuckled. She loved listening to Kennedi talk in her own language. Miki said, "Because her daddy wants to see her."

"Oh. My daddy sees me all da time," Kennedi said.

"I know," Miki said eyeing a displeased Bebe. "Your daddy is a good daddy."

"My know," Kennedi said.

Miki looked in Bebe's eyes. "Stop looking like that. I'll see you Thursday."

"Yeah," he murmured.

Miki hurried Téa to the vehicle. Redd was still calling. Miki turned off the phone. She would pretend that she accidentally powered her phone off and didn't realize it. In the driveway, she cut the phone back on and went through the call log and her texts to make sure nothing was suspicious. She shut it back off.

Letting herself inside Miki plastered a smile on her face to show Redd she was happy to see him. Redd came around the corner. He looked like an albino bull ready to charge.

He ordered, "Téa go to your room."

Miki began to worry. "Why is she going to her room?" She watched Téa scurry along. Miki froze there in the foyer.

"If you ain't at church where the fuck do you think you should be?" Redd asked through gritted teeth. He asked in a calmer tone, "Are you fucking around on me?"

"No," she said nervously.

"What mothafucka's been in your face?"

Miki could turn around real fast and try for the front door. She was sure she could slip out before he reached her, but he had started moving her way. Miki said, "I don't have nobody in my face."

"I'ma ask you one more time. What nigga's been in your face?" He stood directly in front of her.

"When?" she asked nervously. Redd did this often. His paranoia would cause him to make up situations that would allow him to go off and feel justified. However, this time what he was accusing her of was true.

Redd struck her in the face. Miki's head whipped back. She grabbed her face where it started throbbing immediately. He snarled, "Bitch don't play with me. Now tell me who the fuck it is."

Miki began to cry. "I don't know what you're talking about."

He yanked her purse from her and found her phone. "Who the fuck—bitch what the fuck you turn your phone off for?" He struck her again.

"Please Redd. I didn't do anything," Miki cried.

"Why the fuck you turn your phone off?"

"I didn't turn my phone off."

"Why the fuck is it off? Don't play with me Miki!"

"I'm not," she cowered.

He pointed towards their bedroom. "Get in the room."

"Redd...please," she whimpered. Anytime he ordered her to the room, it usually meant at least an hour of torture.

"Getcho ass in the gotdamn room!"

Miki cautiously walked pass him fearing that he would hit her again. Once in the bedroom Miki sat down on the bed. She tried to figure out what she could say or do to get out of this.

Redd was caught up in scrolling through Miki's phone. "I think you fucking with me. And I think you've been deleting shit out of your phone. Why the fuck you lying and playing, Miki?"

Miki couldn't respond with anything. Redd grabbed her by her throat and lifted her from the bed. Immediately, her hands went up to his to try to pry it away. It wasn't budging.

Maliciously, he said, "Let me find out you fucking around. I'm killing you and him. You hear me? Keep mothafuckin playing with me."

He threw her down like she was a ragdoll. Miki rubbed her neck and started crying.

"Whatchu crying for?"

"Because...you always do this, and I don't be doing nothing. I don't deserve this Redd."

"You what?" he asked with incredible disbelief.

"I don't do anyth—" her words were cut off by a blow from Redd.

He barked, "Bitch, I know what the fuck you deserve and what you don't deserve. Fuck you mean...Learn how to shut the fuck up!"

Miki was partially lying on her side ready to protect herself in the fetal position if needed. She tried not to cry as she didn't want to upset him even more.

He eventually left her there. Miki ended up falling asleep only to be awakened by him softly telling her to take her clothes off and get in the bed. He was being soothing. "Baby, go on and get in the bed."

"What time is it?" Miki asked groggily.

"It's night time."

Miki tried to get out of bed. "I gotta cook something."

"That's alright. Mama brought us some plates. Just get in the bed and get some rest. You want something to drink or something?"

Jesus! This man was bipolar. Miki undressed and eased into bed. Something had to give. But every time Miki thought about a future without Redd she saw devastation and chaos.

Chapter 12

The day for Ava's and Larry's anniversary party had finally arrived. When Miki came at Millennium Maxwell House Hotel to help decorate the ballroom for the occasion, Redd video-called her.

"What's up baby?" he asked.

"Nothing," she said making her way over to Kizzie and Maddie. They were in disagreement of how to arrange the tables.

"What have you been doing?"

"Trying to get this ballroom together," she said. She exhaled heavily. She wasn't feeling the greatest that morning. She was nauseated, and she prayed that she wasn't pregnant. At this point, she wouldn't know who the father would be. She had been with Redd and Bebe within days of each other every time. And although Bebe wanted to wear condoms most of the time, there were the two times they didn't use a condom: at the club and the second time they were intimate.

"What's wrong? You don't sound too happy."

When am I ever when it comes to you? "I'm alright. Just feel a little sick."

"I have too. You ain't pregnant, are you?"

"Nah," she said. She didn't want to tell him anything because she doubt she would keep this pregnancy.

"Okay bae. I need you to do the room," he said.

Miki knew exactly what he was asking. Miki repeated, "You need me to do the room. Like a panoramic view?"

"Yeah," he murmured.

"Okay." She flipped the phone facing forward. Maddie and Kizzie both waved.

Kizzie said, "Hey Redd!"

Miki turned around slowly so that he could see there were no men around threatening to take his place or in her face. She slowly and carefully eased the phone back to face her. She said, "Now do yours."

"I can't. Bae, I gotta go. But I love you," he said and ended the call.

Ain't that a bitch, she thought as she made sure her phone was cleared.

"That nigga crazy for real," Bebe said causing Maddie and Kizzie to snicker.

"You're nothing like that are you?" Maddie asked.

"I wouldn't do no bullshit like that," he said.

Miki laughed. "You are crazy. Your ass was right here the whole time moving when I moved."

"I wanted to laugh so bad," Kizzie giggled. "But Redd woulda been asking what's so funny."

Bebe kissed Miki. "Well I know that nigga be trippin'."

"So y'all about to go?" Maddie asked.

"We'll be back though. Just going out to grab a bite to eat," Miki said.

"Okay. Y'all be careful," Maddie said.

Miki and Bebe drove to Hendersonville to enjoy a nice lunch at Cheddars. Miki was paranoid and kept looking over her shoulders to make sure there was no one there that would recognize her.

"Miki, stop worrying about that," Bebe was telling her. "If somebody see you, fuck it. I got you. I mean it."

"I know. But you have no idea how Redd's mind work. He's not going to make leaving his ass easy."

"Stop obsessing over that. But can I ask you a question?"

"You just did. No more questions," she laughed.

Bebe gave her a blank look but a smile quickly formed. "See I love when you smile or laugh. I wanna see you happy."

Miki blushed and focused on her food.

Bebe asked, "What made you stay in the first place?"

"With Redd?"

Bebe nodded.

"I ain't gon lie. He had bank. I wasn't hurting for no money or anything 'cause my mama and stepdad took real good care of us. It's just back then a thug that was balling was appealing to me. Redd didn't show his true colors until much later. But I was gullible, young and naïve."

"You know my sister kinda going through the same thing and I guess that's why I'm so passionately against it. My mama went through it with my dad when he was home. I always said I wanted to be nothing like him."

"Do you think watching your mother go through it kinda affected your sister and that's why she's going through it?"

"I don't know. Marvin took good care of her and their boys. My sister was like you. She didn't have to work. She was a housewife, but she done moved out and got her own place.

He's trying to convince her to move back home."

"Well at least she had the courage to leave."

"You'll find that courage too."

"You think so."

"I know so. Keep fucking with me you'll get there. I won't rest until you do," he said throwing her a charismatic smile.

His smile made Miki blush. Being Bebe's woman would be nice. He was everything she wished Redd was. She asked, "Where's your children?"

"With my mama and my sister."

"We gotta do a play date for Téa and Kennedi."

"Me and Kennedi can be available whenever."

"Those two are a trip. They would made good stepsisters."

Bebe smiled knowingly. "So, what are you trying to say?"

Miki grinned sneakily. "Nothing."

"Mmm hmm," he hummed.

"You want more kids?" she asked.

"Yeah. I would love to have another baby with the woman I make my wife. You want more?"

Miki thought of her impending fate. She knew she was pregnant. The signs were there. She was over a week late but her period act funny at times. She had periods as close as fourteen days within each other and as long as forty days apart. This one however was late, and her breast really hurt and there was an absence of cramps. She answered, "Not at this time. Not with Redd at least."

"Oh. What if things got real serious with you and me?"

“I don’t think it would matter then. As long as you’re not treating me like the way Redd does.”

“Never that. I would never put my hands on you like that. Well at least not in that way. I’d like to put my hands on you in many other ways though,” he said with a hint of seduction.

Miki smiled, “I’m sure you would.”

“Hurry up and eat girl so we can take care of business.”

“What business?”

“Don’t play dumb.”

Miki loved the way Bebe made her feel. She knew she needed to do something and do it soon.

Miki was having such a good time at the party with Bebe she never once thought about Redd. Bebe had turned out to be the life of the party. As much as Miki tried to remain cool and casual by not being under Bebe, he wouldn’t let her get too far from her. He danced with her, with her sisters, Kat, both Téa and Kennedi at the same time, her mother, her aunts and her grandmother. He interacted with her boy cousins, uncles, stepdad, and his male family members. When little nine-year-old Tyiesha got up to do a song dedication to Ava and Larry she was nervous and forgot the words. Bebe was right there giving the girl praises and encouraging words as he helped her with the words to Amazing by Luther Vandross. After two hours Bebe was everybody’s favorite person.

The feeling it left Miki with was overwhelming. She felt happier than she had in a while. If only she could have that feeling forever. However, that sensation was short-lived when Miki realized Redd’s sister Montiece and his mother Mona was there. Her heart sunk.

"Who invited them?" Miki asked.

Kizzie stood there wearing a sheepish grin. "I'm guilty. I didn't think they would show though."

Miki gave Kizzie a devastated look with an utterance of despair. "Why?"

"Well I ran into Montiece and told her about it. I had no idea you would be inviting Bebe," Kizzie explained.

"Don't be mad at her, Miki. It was innocent," Maddie said.

Montiece saw Miki and walked over. "Hey ladies."

"Hey," Maddie said halfheartedly. She didn't care for any of the Jeffries. They were all conniving and vindictive.

"Look at you, Miki," Montiece commented. "You look good."

"Thanks," Miki said with a forced smile.

"My brother ain't' here?" Montiece asked.

"Naw. He's out of town," she said. She added, "Again."

Montiece looked out to the dance floor and scanned the rest of the room. "It's a lot of people here. This is a nice party. Maddie, I know you done that cake."

"You know I did," Maddie said as her husband Gary came over.

"C'mon woman. You owe me a dance," Gary said.

"Well ladies, I must go and dance with my husband," she said as Gary led her away.

Montiece asked, "Who's that?"

Miki and Kizzie looked in the direction Montiece was looking. Miki just knew she was talking about Bebe, but she was hoping she wasn't.

"In the orange and grey plaid shirt," Montiece said.

Bebe looked up and saw the ladies looking. He flashed a smile and began to walk over. Shit! Miki thought.

"Uhm...he's a friend of the family," Kizzie said shooting Miki a quick glance.

Bebe didn't give much thought to Montiece standing there. He was focused in on Miki. She tried to shake her head at him and gestured towards Montiece with her eyes. He didn't see it. He said, "Hey baby. Come on and dance with me. I see Gary finally got Maddie out there."

Miki's eyes widened. Kizzie cleared her throat and said, "I'll dance with you. Redd's sister here was talking to Miki."

Bebe looked at Montiece noticing her for the first time. She was light and bright like Redd. She had the same green eyes too. He looked at Miki and saw her pleading with her eyes. He reached his hand out to Kizzie, "C'mon babygirl."

Miki didn't miss the flash of displeasure written across Bebe's face. She eyed his bowed legs as he walked away with Kizzie.

"What was that about?" Montiece asked.

"I don't know but Toni gon' get his ass," Miki said trying to make light of the situation.

"Did he call you 'baby'?"

"Naw. Probably babygirl or by name," Miki lied.

Montiece gave Miki a skeptical look. She looked out at the

dance floor where Bebe was. “He’s a cutie. I love a man with bow legs.”

Miki said nothing.

Montiece asked, “You think he got a woman?”

“I’m not sure.”

Montiece looked back at Miki. She smacked her lips before asking, “How are you and my brother doing?”

“We’re doing okay.”

“That’s good. Well I’m gonna go grab me something to eat.”

Do that, Miki thought.

Minutes later Bebe sat down at the table Miki decided to sit at. He asked, “Did you know she was gonna be here?”

“No.”

“Is her being here gonna make you not wanna dance with me again?”

“Yeah. She will hurry up and run back to Redd telling him everything.”

“Let her. I don’t want her to ruin your good mood. You’ve been enjoying yourself since we’ve been here.”

“I know but I don’t want Redd coming with some shit,” Miki said solemnly.

“Baby, let’s just get this over with.”

“No Bebe. And I’m not gonna keep talking about that. I’m tired of talking about it.”

“Okay,” he said with defeat. He asked, “So will you be coming home with me tonight?”

“Yeah. Of course,” she smiled.

Chapter 13

It was Halloween. Bebe and Miki had been seeing each other for a little over two months. Bebe had never been so in love. He loved everything about Miki. He loved the way she laughed, smiled, even when she cried. He loved to cuddle with her early Sunday mornings. The only problem was Bebe hated the rules. Thursdays and Sundays weren't enough for him. He wanted all of Miki. He wanted her from Sunday to Sunday.

The evening was enjoyable. Miki and Téa spent Halloween night going from door to door with Bebe, BJ, Kennedi, Maddie, Gary and their three kids. Téa and Kennedi were terrified of everything. Miki tried to console them while Bebe, BJ, Gary and Gary Jr. laughed their asses off.

Kennedi got mad at her father. She asked angrily, "Whatchu funny at Daddy?"

That caused more laughter. Téa said in her meek little voice, "Mommy, I'm ready to go home."

"Home or Auntie Maddie's?"

Téa grinned sneakily, "Kennedi's!"

Bebe looked at Miki with a smile. "Téa has spoken."

Miki gave him a desperate look. He always did that. He played on the kids' wants to get what he wanted out of Miki. He knew Miki had a soft spot for Kennedi's and Téa's friendship. She looked down at Téa, "Maybe for a little while."

Kennedi was excited. She and Téa shared a tight hug.

"Does this mean you're coming over?" Bebe asked.

“Yeah,” Miki said softly. She looked at the time on her phone. It was still early. The girls didn’t need to be out that late. They still had school the following morning. Miki told Redd what she would be doing which was taking Téa trick or treating. He didn’t have any objections. He hadn’t bother to call Miki either. Miki could only assume he was with one of his girlfriends. She didn’t care. She could be with her baby.

After spending forty minutes down at Maddie’s Miki joined Bebe at his house. As the kids went off to play Bebe asked, “Are you sure you’ll be okay. I don’t want him all in your face.”

“I’m fine,” she said. She walked into the living room and sat down on the couch. Bebe walked around and stretched out on the couch resting his head in her lap. Miki started stroking his hair. “Bebe?”

“Huh?”

“We gotta come up with a plan.”

“I think I have one in mind already but I gotta talk to a few people first,” Bebe said.

“Don’t have him killed Bebe,” Miki said.

“I’m not that type of person Miki,” he said. He closed his eyes enjoying the sweet feel of her lap and her touch. Being near Miki was comforting. Every hour, every minute he got to spend with her he cherished.

Miki closed her eyes and let her head fall back. Unable to resist the heaviness of sleep Miki drifted away. With both of them sleeping, time began to slip by. The kids were clueless as they played along with Shadow.

A trick-or-treater rang the doorbell. That was what

awakened them. Miki panicked when she realized that it was completely dark. She felt for her phone. "Oh my God! Where's my phone?"

"Calm down, Miki. It's only eight-thirty," Bebe said soothingly.

"I haven't cooked anything," she said frantically. "Téa!"

Téa and Kennedi came running into the living room with Shadow behind them. "C'mon baby, we gotta go."

"I'll drive you around there," Bebe said.

"No, we'll walk," Miki said. Having Bebe drop her off at her sister's house was too risky at this time.

"Baby, it's dark out there," Bebe said.

"It's just around the corner. We'll be okay."

Miki was so glad she didn't let Bebe bring her back to her sister's house. Redd was waiting outside in his SUV. She knew she was in trouble. She didn't even bother trying to avoid him. She walked right up to his truck.

"Where the fuck you been?" Redd asked.

"Me and Téa were still trick-or-treating," she said.

"Where is your phone?" he asked coolly.

"I left it here."

"Get your shit and c'mon to this house," he said.

Téa held up her glow in the dark candy bucket. "Look how much I got Daddy. I gotta lot."

He didn't acknowledge Téa. He just stared coldly at Miki.

Miki grabbed Téa by the hand, "C'mon Téa so we can say bye to Auntie Maddie and Uncle Gary."

Miki was surprised that Redd wasn't trying to put his hands on her when they go to the house. He was just a control freak and wanted to control her every move. If he felt like she should be in the house by a specific time, then that's what he wanted to see.

While Redd was in the bathroom his cell phone rang. Miki looked at the screen and it was from a private number. Redd called from the bathroom. "Bring me my phone."

The call ended but it started ringing back immediately. Again, private number. For the hell of it Miki answered it. "Hello?"

"Uhm...may I speak to Tanya?" a girl asked hesitantly.

Miki scoffed, "You don't want Tanya. You want Redd. Here he go."

"Didn't I tell you to hand me my phone?" Redd said coming out of the bathroom.

Miki extended the phone out to him. "One of your hoes on the phone."

Redd snatched the phone from her and cleared his line.

Miki sat down on the bed and began channel surfing. "I don't even know why you continue to pretend as if I don't know you ain't fucking around."

"Shut up, Miki. I ain't tryna hear your shit tonight," he said going to the closet.

"Where you going?" she asked.

"Don't worry about it."

Miki grew angry. "Redd, you came to my sister's house to make me leave and come home; and now you're about to leave back out."

"Who said I was leaving at first? But I will now so I don't have to hear this shit."

Wryly, Miki laughed. "I wonder which one was that. Laila? It kinda sounded like Tamika."

Redd came out of the closet and looked at Miki with his eyebrows deep in a furrow. "Let me ask you this, Miki. If it is another bitch, whatchu gon do about it?"

Miki didn't answer. This was a trick question. No matter how she wanted to reply, it would be a loss either way. Her best bet was to be quiet.

"That's what the fuck I thought," he sneered. "Now shut the fuck up."

Chapter 14

Two weeks later, Bebe found himself frustrated. He hadn't heard from Miki in two weeks and it was killing him.

According to Merriam-Webster dictionary the term addiction was a strong and harmful need to regularly have something such as a drug or do something such as gambling and/or an unusually great interest in something or a need to do or have something. So, was it safe to say Bebe was addicted to Miki? He needed her. He wanted her in his life. His dick fit perfectly in her pussy. She made him feel good spiritually and emotionally. When he was not with her he didn't feel like himself. She completed a part of him that he didn't know existed.

"What are you over there thinking about brother?" Bless asked. They sat in his mother's den.

"My baby," he mumbled.

"Kennedi?"

"No. Miki."

"Your baby?" Bless teased. "This sounds serious."

"My feelings are serious," he said. "And right now, I'm sick 'cause I hadn't seen her or been with her in almost two weeks."

"This is the girl with the situation, right?"

Bebe nodded.

"She hasn't left yet?"

"That's the problem. We've been seeing each other for three months now. I would have thought that she would be at a point now to make a choice."

"It may take a while. It depends on how scared she is of this man."

"I want her away from him. Her and her daughter."

"Is her daughter his child?"

He nodded.

"I can understand her dilemma because of course I went through it," Bless said.

"I can't understand it. I treat her so much better than he treat her. You would think she would just leave."

"She's afraid of him Bebe. More than likely she's scared of what he might do to not just her but everybody around her." Bless pointed out.

Bebe's phone rang. He hoped it was Miki. It was Dinky. "Yeah?"

"Whatchu bout to get into nigga?" Dinky said playfully.

"Nothing," Bebe mumbled.

"Shit go out to Abstract with me," Dinky suggested. "Bring your woman too."

"What woman?"

"Aw hell. You don't mess with ol' girl no more?" Dinky said with disappointment.

"Yeah but she got that situation. What time you tryna get to Abstract?"

"Ten."

"A'ight."

Joyce came into the den as Bebe ended the call. “Hey Mama,” he said. His tone was somber, and he knew his mother would pick up on it.

“What’s wrong big head boy?” she asked. She took a seat beside him on the couch.

“I don’t know what to do,” Bebe sighed.

“About what?”

“Miki.”

“Didn’t I tell you about that?” she chided.

“But she said she wants to leave him.”

“Look, she’s gonna have to get to a place where she’s tired Bebe. And until she do you need to fall back.”

“How can I fall back? I love this woman.”

“You may love her. I’m sure you do. But you can’t be with everybody you love. Furthermore, you can’t save her Bebe. You can’t convince her. She’s gotta come to these conclusions on her own. My advice to you is walk away from it, love her from a distance and pray for her.”

“I hear ya Mama.”

“Hear me loud and clear. I know you Bebe. You got that little hot temper. Eventually you’ll wanna go over there and fight that man. He’s a coward and he won’t fight fair with a man. So, you’ll either end up in jail or dead. It’s not your place to confront that man either. She cheating on him with you.”

“But I confront Marvin all the time.”

Joyce shot Bless a look. “Yeah. For your sister. And look at her situation. You see how long it took for her to finally get the courage to leave. Look at me and your Daddy’s situation. I finally left him, and the nigga died." She chuckled on that last part.

"Mama, that's not funny," Bless interjected.

Bebe said to Bless, "Maybe you and her need to become friends so you can convince her to do what you did."

"I wanna get to know her anyway. Any woman to have my twin so gone is worth getting to know," Bless said.

Joyce said, "See if she can come over for Thanksgiving."

"I'll ask her. She might be able to escape for a little bit." He knew what Miki's answer would be, but he would try his luck anyway.

That night Bebe and Dinky let Deja and Cyn hang out with them at the club. All night Cyn had been under Bebe. She showed jealousy if he talked with any other girl. Bebe thought Cyn was so cute.

Physically, Cyn was his ideal woman. She was educated and had an excellent job with a sixty-thousand-dollar salary as an MRI technologist. She drove a nice car and always kept up. She had no kids at the age of twenty-seven. She was a good catch. Bebe was tired of playing with her though.

"There you go again," Bebe said to Cyn.

She grinned sneakily. "What are you talking about now?"

"The way you looking at me. Whatchu want Cyn?"

"What's up with you and that girl?"

"Miki?"

"That's her name? Then yeah, her."

“Nothing,” he answered. Of course, he wasn’t going to tell her how serious he felt about Miki because Bebe still wanted to keep his options open just in case things didn’t work out between him and Miki.

Deja came over pulling on Cyn, “Girl c’mon. Go with me to the bar.”

As Cyn got up Bebe reached out and smacked her on the ass. She smiled back at him. If he kept it up, he knew he would be getting that later.

Abstract was a laid back grown and sexy lounge club. It was where the ones with deep pockets frequented to show off just how deep their pockets were. Bebe didn’t have deep pockets but he was privy to all of the VIP treatment. He was related to one of the owners of the club.

“Look at that bitch right there,” Dinky said under his breath. He was eyeing a scantily clad female across the way.

“Go holla at her nigga,” Bebe said casually.

“He wouldn’t know what to do with that,” Keonte joked.

“Like you would,” Dinky said cutting his eyes. “I bet I get her number. Might be even fucking later.”

Bebe shook his head laughing as Dinky walked away to make his approach.

“That nigga stupid,” Keonte said. He sat forward in his chair. “So, what’s up with you and ol’ girl?”

“You talking about Miki?”

“Yeah.”

Bebe half shrugged.

“You know she here with ya boy,” Keonte said. He spoke as

if it was a secret.

“She here?” Bebe asked looking around the crowded club.

“I thought you seen her. They on the other side.”

Bebe sprung from his chair because he had to see this. How could she bring her ass to a club and hadn’t bother to once call him?

Bebe didn’t have to get up that close to be able to tell it was Miki. She was with Redd, Kat, and a few others Bebe had seen around them. She didn’t look distraught, frightened, or anything. She looked like she was having a good time. Bebe was disgusted.

“Fuck that bitch,” Bebe said under his breath. He said fuck her, but he couldn’t turn away. It was heart-wrenching watching her enjoying herself as if Bebe didn’t exist in her world. He watched her as she and Kat departed from the group and headed towards the bar. It was out of Redd’s direct view so Bebe decided to approach Miki.

“So, this is how it is now?” he asked her directly.

She was startled when she saw him. She glanced Redd’s way before she spoke. “It isn’t what you think it is.”

“What the fuck that mean, Miki?” Bebe asked angrily.

Kat stared at both of them knowing that if they caused a scene it would attract Redd over.

“It means I’m only here because of Kat,” she said.

“And you couldn’t call me?”

“I couldn’t. You know my situation,” she said.

“Yeah I know your situation but two weeks. I hadn’t seen you and barely heard from you. Then I see you here with that nigga. This is fucked up, Miki."

"I'm just going through something right now, Bebe," Miki explained.

"Can you come over here with me for a minute?" Bebe asked.

"So y'all can fight?" Miki asked incredulously.

"That nigga ain't tryna fight no man," he said. He went to grab Miki by the arm, but she pulled away.

"Excuse me ma'am, but is he bothering you?" a deep voice asked. Bebe spun around ready to cuss the imposing man out but started grinning when he realized who it was.

"What's up, nigga," Bebe said as he exchanged a one-shoulder brotherly hug and handshake with the taller man.

"Nothing. I see you over here harassing women. What's up ladies?" Abe said looking over at a now smiling Miki. Abe said to her, "You have to excuse my cousin. I know he was raised right but it didn't stick with him."

"Shut up ol' yella ass nigga," Bebe kidded. He noticed Miki about to walk away with Kat. He grabbed Miki this time. "Where you going? You staying with me."

Miki allowed him to pull her close to him. He thought her change in behavior had everything to do with Abe's presence. Abe was eye candy for women. His fair skin, icy blue eyes, build, pretty hair and poise had an effect on women that literally hypnotized them. Abe was also the co-owner of Abstract.

"Let me go so he won't be all upset," she said. Not wanting to cause a scene Bebe let her loose. He and Abe watched the two women walk off.

Abe asked, "You know she got a man that's here right?"

"You know him?"

"His shop is in my north plaza," Abe answered.

"Fuck that nigga," Bebe uttered.

"Be careful with that," Abe said. "But you know I got your back if anything ever goes down."

Bebe nodded.

"I gotta go. It was nice bumping into you. You need to come out to the house more often," Abe said as he walked off.

Bebe didn't want to push the issue with Miki nor did he want to appear desperate. He tried to sit back with Deja and Cyn while attempting to watch Miki from a distance. It soured his mood and he was ready to leave.

Bebe went and grabbed Dinky ending his enjoyable evening to let him know he was leaving. Since Bebe was his ride Dinky had to call it a night too. He helped Bebe with the two drunk girls outside as they made it to Bebe's truck.

The two girls leaned on each other, using one another to keep themselves up. Deja felt something wet drip on her face. Her eyes widened, "Am I crying and don't know it?"

Cyn laughed. "Bitch, that's the rain."

Deja said, "I feel a little sick."

"You bet not throw up in my truck either," Bebe said as he got in the driver's side. Dinky held the door open for the two girls to get in. Before Deja could climb in she vomited.

"Aw! Hell naw!" Dinky exclaimed with disgust. "She got some on my shoes."

"I'm sorry Dink," Deja mumbled.

"Deja don't get in my truck," Bebe warned. "Not if your drunk ass still gotta throw up."

Cyn started to laugh uncontrollably.

"Drunk asses," Bebe said under his breath.

Cyn let her arms dangle over Bebe's seat. She said to him, "I'ma fuck you tonight."

"Sorry babygirl, but I don't fuck drunk pussy," he chuckled.

"Fuck you Bebe!" Cyn yelled.

Bebe laughed even more. Dinky shook his head. "You ain't right."

Bebe took Cyn and Deja back to Deja's place. He and Dinky had to help both of them into the apartment. Once back in the truck Bebe asked, "Which one: Cyn or Miki?"

Dinky snorted a laugh. "Serious?"

"Who would you pick?"

"Cyn. No questions asked."

Bebe was surprised by Dinky's answer. He asked, "Why?"

"Cyn ain't got a crazy ass domestic violence ass baby daddy attached to her."

Bebe grinned. "You got that right. Cyn or Stefani?"

"Hell naw! Just get you a new piece. All them bitches that was on you tonight. I know you got somebody's number."

"Yeah but I'm looking for a wife."

"Stefani ain't it. Cyn would be alright if she toned it down a bit with the clubs."

“I can mold Cyn.”

“Mold my ass. She gon end up molding your ass,” Dinky joked.

“I doubt that.”

“Well why couldn’t you mold Miki?”

“She’s an exception. She wasn’t meant to be molded. Her baby daddy done already done that.”

“So, what’s up between y’all two now?”

“Same shit.”

Dinky grinned knowingly. “Ah. Now I know why you talking about Cyn.”

“Yeah,” he said as thoughts of Miki roamed in his head. He said, “I really love that girl too.”

Chapter 15

Miki knew Bebe was sour about not hearing from her or seeing her. It wasn't fun for her either. She missed him terribly but since school was out for two whole weeks what excuse could she give Redd especially if he had his other kids at the house at different times. Miki couldn't get a break. That's what she wanted to explain to Bebe when she saw him at Abstract. She hadn't been avoiding him on purpose. She just hoped he wasn't ready to move on.

"So whatchu gon do baby?" Redd asked. They laid lazily in bed next to one another.

His question brought Miki back from her thoughts. "About what?"

"Thanksgiving. You wanna go to my granny's or are you going to your sister's house?"

"If I go to Maddie's are you coming?"

"Probably not. I might stop by to speak but that's it. You know they don't like me."

"Well what do you want me to do?"

"I mean you can do either one. I know how you like to go over to your sister house and act retarded with them."

Miki smiled. "So, you're saying it'll be okay if I go to my sister's house for Thanksgiving by myself?"

Redd smiled back. "Yes. Why you cheesing?"

"Cause...I can't believe you can be nice sometimes."

"I'm trying," he said. He pecked her on the lips. He pulled

her into him and held her tight. He kissed her on the forehead. "I love you. I really wanna do right by you and Téa. Please give me that chance."

Miki wrapped her arms around his torso. This was the Redd that she loved. This was the Redd that she wouldn't dare look at another man for. This was the man that she loved going places with. She loved for him to come home to her. She loved for him to make love to her. There was no doubt that Redd had a piece of her heart. But was it enough to let go of the love developing between her and Bebe?

"What can I do to fix us?" he asked.

"I just want some peace. I'm tired of you hitting on me and barking at me all of the time. You go through my phone constantly 'cause you don't trust me. I don't even be doing shit."

"Niggas be calling your phone though."

"So. You got women calling you at all times of the day."

He was quiet. Miki said nothing.

Redd finally said, "I'll get help. We can go to counseling. You know I love you. I wanna do right by you but you know I got this temper. You be doing shit that make me mad."

"But Redd, you gotta learn to control your temper."

"That's why I said I'll get help Miki. But I need your help too, baby."

Miki could hear the desperation in his voice. Redd did need help. Maybe one day he could be a great man for someone. He was damn good at providing. There was nothing she or Téa wanted for. He had been very good at putting Miki and Téa first. He was a decent father to his other five kids as well. Redd had the potential to be a good man. For a long time, Miki always thought that if she left Redd he would go off and be a better man to another woman than he had ever been to her. She was waiting around to see if he would ever turn into this better man for her.

"Where is all of this coming from Redd?" Miki asked curiously.

"I just don't wanna lose you. Sometimes I think I've already have."

"Nah. I'm still here. I just want you to be happy. When you're happy it makes the whole house happy. You're the man. You're supposed to be the head. Me and Téa should be a reflection of you."

"I get what you're saying. I'ma try Miki. I really am."

"Okay. I'm hold it to you," Miki teased.

Redd looked her up and down. "You still bleeding?"

Miki tried to keep the smile plastered to her face, but she found herself feeling awkward. She had been lying to Redd telling him that she was hurting and bleeding bad. She explained to him that she thought she had fibroids and it was bloating her stomach. Truth was she was eleven weeks pregnant with a due date in June. Her conception date went back to the time when she had sex with Bebe in the club and when Redd snapped on her violently taking sex from her. Miki had no idea who the father was because they were literally within hours of one another although Redd did pull out just to shoot his cum all over her.

"It's slowing down a little. I gotta go for an ultrasound next week though. The doctor wants to confirm the fibroids," she lied.

"Aw. Well, I'm about to get ready to head out," he said hopping up from the bed.

Miki knew that also meant he was going to go to one of his women's house to satisfy his sexual need. She didn't care.

As soon as he left Miki called Bebe.

"Hello?"

"Hey," she said meekly.

"Hey," he said dryly.

"Do you have to sound like that?"

"How should I sound? Happy because you finally called me?"

"Uhm yeah," she said trying to make the moment light.

"Where's your man?"

"He's gone. But I was calling to ask you what are your plans for tomorrow morning?"

"I'll be over my mama's. She wanted me to invite you over."

"Ah tell her thanks for the invite but I can't. But I could see you tomorrow morning before the day gets started."

"Let me guess. He'll be gone during that time."

"Well he's letting me go to my sister's house instead of going to his granny's house. He said he'll be by my sister's house later though. That's why I can't be gone all day. But I thought since you're right around the corner I could come see you early in the day."

The feeling of being used settled over Bebe. "Are you using me Miki?"

She laughed as if what he said was absurd. “No. Why would you say that?”

“Tomorrow when you come by my house...what are your plans?”

She was hesitant in her reply. “Why are you being difficult?”

“I’m not. You know this isn’t the easiest thing for me. You got me waiting around on you. And—”

“Don’t you wanna see me?” she interrupted.

“Yeah, I want to. I miss you. But...”

“But what? Bebe you knew my situation.”

“I know so I can only be mad at myself.”

“What are you trying to say?”

“I’m saying...I need more baby.”

Miki contemplated his statement. He needed more. She did too. She was in love with Bebe and knew he was getting tired of this. He just didn’t understand. Miki was sure if she left Redd he would come after her and Bebe. Somebody wouldn’t survive.

“Give me more time baby,” Miki said softly.

“How much more time?”

“I don’t know. But can I see you tomorrow morning?”

“I guess so.”

“Okay. I’ll see you then. Love you.”

“Love you too.”

Chapter 16

As bad as Bebe had wanted to see Miki he knew he had to do what he was about to do. His mother was right. He would have to sever ties with Miki. He needed what he couldn't have with Miki. When he first set out to be the nigga on the side his every intention was to love her enough to compel her to leave Redd. She wasn't budging. She didn't trust Bebe to protect her. Miki saw it as riskier to leave over staying.

Miki showed up at his house like she said she would early Thursday morning. "Hey love," she said sweetly. She pecked him on the lips.

"Hey," he said. He was happy to see her because it had been a while. "You look nice as always."

"Thanks," she said removing her coat. She frowned. "What's wrong? You don't look too thrilled to see me."

"I...am," he said with hesitance. He didn't bother to move from his living room. He leaned up against the arm of his sofa and folded his arms across his chest.

Still holding her coat, Miki walked upon him searching his eyes for an answer. "What is it Bebe?"

He sighed heavily and unfolded his arms. "I can't do this anymore."

"Can't do what?"

"Us. This."

"Bebe..." her voice trailed as she wrapped her mind around what he was trying to say. "Are you breaking up with me?"

Bebe let out a cynical laugh. “Breakup? What’s to break up if we’re not even together?”

“You know what I mean. So, you don’t wanna see me anymore?”

“I can’t see you anymore,” he said.

“You can’t, or you won’t?”

“I won’t. Not like this anymore.”

There was a pause as Miki looked everywhere but at Bebe’s piercing gaze. He was trying to read her and see exactly how she was feeling. He asked, “Can you understand where I’m coming from?”

“I guess,” she mumbled. She kept her eyes lowered.

“You don’t sound like—”

She interrupted, “I’m fine. I knew it would come to this anyway. So, is this the last time I will see you?”

Bebe nodded.

Miki sighed with defeat. She thought about how miserable life had been with Redd. She looked forward to seeing Bebe. He was the highlight of her week.

Bebe couldn’t reveal how he really felt about his decision. Inside he was torn. He loved Miki. He would even make her his wife but that wasn’t the life she was ready for.

Silent tears streamed down Miki’s cheeks. She tried to be quiet with her sniffles as she stared down at the floor. She looked up at him and he could see the streaks on her face. He looked at her lovingly but with desperation in his eyes.

“Miki, please leave him. That’s all you gotta do,” Bebe said softly. “Please don’t cry either.”

Miki grew angry and frustrated. It seemed insensitive how Bebe didn't try to console or comfort her. He now treated her like she was just some girl he was acquainted with. "What you expect me to do? You think this shit is easy for me? It ain't, Bebe."

"I'm not saying it is."

"I can't believe you're leaving me," she spat.

"I'm not leaving you. You made a choice. I shoulda accepted your choice the first time you made me aware of it."

"What choice?"

"You chose being with Redd just like you're doing now."

"It's not a choice! What don't y'all get?"

"What I get is that you care more about him and the consequences he'll suffer if you stand up to him than you do about your own wellbeing. Don't you wanna be happy and worry-free, Miki?"

"So, what are you suggesting I do Bebe?"

"Shoot his ass or call the police on him."

"I can't send him back to prison. I just can't."

"That's what I'm talking about. Fuck his freedom. What about yours? I get so tired of seeing bruises on you. What kind of man am I to sit back and let him do this to you? Since you don't want to leave him it's best if I separate myself from this whole situation."

Miki nodded her acknowledgment. "I get it Bebe...Well I guess I'll see you around."

He tried to reach out to touch her, hug her...anything. She jerked away from him. "Don't," she spat.

"I can't get a hug?"

Miki slipped her coat back on and headed for the door.

"Miki," he called.

"Just let me go," Miki cried. She opened the door and slipped out.

Bebe wanted to open the door and yell out, "I'm just playing. Get back in here," but he knew this was the best thing to do. He didn't deserve to be some side piece when he was "the only man she need" material. There were plenty of women that would be willing to be his woman. But he knew that those women were not Miki. However, he had to move on.

Miki couldn't rationalize in her head why she had allowed things to fall as they did. If she wanted to get away from Redd being with Bebe would have been her opportunity. Now she felt foolish for even attempting to have something with another man. She didn't have the courage it took to leave Redd. She wasted her time and Bebe's time. Well her time wasn't wasted because she enjoyed every moment she shared with Bebe. She wanted to keep Bebe in her life because he balanced everything out for her. He was the joy of her week. However, she felt she needed to be there for Redd.

"I think you're dumb," Kat huffed.

"I know what you're thinking," Miki said with a roll of the eyes. "You've told me plenty of times."

"I think you're scared," Kat said. "You're afraid of moving forward with a real relationship."

"So are you. You sit around and take Ox's shit."

"Don't be flipping this shit on me," Kat said. "You had a perfectly good man in your face that treated you like a queen."

"Yeah for now. Who knows what he would have acted like in nine months."

"So now you're gonna base every man off of Redd's crusty ass."

"No."

"Then what is this?"

"My life," Miki said. She was growing annoyed with this conversation.

"If I was Bebe I wouldn't have a good thing to say about you. You basically used that man. You treated him as if he was nothing ever to you."

"No, I didn't."

"I never thought you were but you're selfish as fuck," Kat said matter of factly.

"No, I'm not. If Redd is willing to change and be a better man why should I not give him an opportunity? I got time invested with him. With him I know what I'm working with. Bebe, not so much. And he has a temper on him too. Why would I leave one mess to get with another one?"

Kat stared at Miki in an unbelieving blank manner. "Something is wrong with you. One minute you're in love with Bebe and he's this and he's that. Now you tryna make him out to be another Redd."

"Why are you so bothered and against me?" Miki questioned.

"Because this is stupid!" Kat exclaimed. She got up from

her couch. "Shit I wished I had met Bebe first."

"And done what? You wouldn't have left Ox completely alone."

Kat gave it some thought. "I only fuck with Ox because of the money. As soon as I meet someone new I'm cutting his ass completely the fuck off."

"Like Ox gonna let you do that," Miki said doubtfully.

"If I give the nigga no choice."

Miki wondered what Redd was up to. He hadn't exploded on her in a while. He had been nothing but loving. Miki blurted, "I'm pregnant."

"What?" Kat gasped.

"I'm pregnant. According to my due date my conception date was around the time of that bathroom incident with Bebe. But Redd also had sex with me that night. I wanna tell Bebe but I don't want it to seem like I'm telling him to keep him. You know what I'm saying. I don't wanna be one of those girls."

"So, you don't know who the daddy could be?"

"I can't be one hundred percent sure, but Redd pulled out because he know I ain't on birth control. Bebe usually use condoms but we were caught up in the moment."

"Are you gonna tell him?" Kat asked.

"I don't know."

"Are you keeping it?" Kat asked.

"I'm not doing an abortion Kat. I just can't."

"So whatchu gon do when that baby come out looking like Bebe and not like Redd?"

“I don’t know. Redd will probably kill me and the baby.”

“Don’t say that,” Kat said. She shook her head. Kat confessed, “I’ve been seeing Dwayne.”

“Dwayne? Dwayne who?”

“Toya’s Dwayne. Ox and Redd’s friend Dwayne.”

Miki grimaced and sucked air through her teeth. “That’s not good Kat. What the fuck are you thinking? What is he thinking?”

Kat shrugged. “It just happened. He came over one night. Things got heated right away. We went at it. Ox must’ve been at some bitch house because Dwayne didn’t feel worried about Ox possibly coming by. We got to talking shit and one thing lead to another.”

“Dang,” Miki mumbled. “And I thought my shit was fucked up.”

Kat exhaled heavily with despair. “Miki, we gotta get our shit together.”

Chapter 17

Although Cyn was on top of him rocking her body back and forward Bebe could only think of Miki. He'd rather it be Miki riding him. He loved that woman and couldn't get enough of her. Cyn was filling a void that Miki left empty.

"Do this pussy feel good?" Cyn asked.

Her question snapped Bebe back to the task at hand. He wanted it to be over with. He pulled Cyn down to his chest and held her around her back as he thrust inside her over and over, deep and fast until he found himself cumming.

Cyn eased off his dick and fell to the bed beside him. "That was good baby."

Bebe mumbled something unintelligible. He got up removing the condom. He took it the bathroom to flush it in the toilet. He didn't trust Cyn. He caught her trying to do something with one of his used condoms one time. When he called her on it she played it off like she was just looking at it and was about to flush it. He let it slide.

Giving in to temptation with Cyn had been easy. She happened to be there at the right time when Bebe was trying to get over Miki. Bebe was reluctant to take his and Cyn's friendship to that place but Cyn wasn't backing down. She threw the pussy on him. Did he want a full-fledged relationship with Cyn? No. Was he afraid that he had led her on to think so? Yes. Now he had to get himself out of this situation.

After taking a piss, Bebe rejoined Cyn in his bed. As soon as he got comfortable he asked, "Cyn, what do you want out of this?"

"Like with us?" she asked.

"Yeah."

"Honestly...I want something special with you Bebe. You know I've been feeling you forever."

"Yeah I know. What if I told you I wasn't ready for a real relationship?"

"What are you ready for then?"

"Just being friends."

"So why are you talking to me about this?"

"Because I've seen some of your posts on Facebook."

"Those are innocent. I wasn't really saying anything with doing that."

"Yeah, but other people think that we're serious."

Cyn turned to face him. "So, we weren't getting serious?"

"It was and that's why I want to slow things down. You're here a lot. I don't usually do that."

Cyn smiled, "That's because you ain't never had a woman like me."

"No, it's because I'm slipping."

Cyn frowned. "Slipping?" Then the thought came to her. "Oh! This is about Miki."

This time Bebe frowned. "Why do you say that?"

"You were using me as your rebound girl to help you get over Miki."

"I wasn't using you," he lied. He was truthful when he said,

"I do like you. And you know we've had this attraction between us for a while even before Miki came into the picture."

Cyn said nothing.

Bebe thought about Miki. He wanted to see her. He needed to see her. He grabbed his cell phone from the nightstand to see the time. "Don't you need to be getting ready for work?"

"You're trying to kick me out now," she said. She got out of bed.

Bebe could only catch a quick glance of her ass as the t-shirt she wore fell over her body. He didn't know why she kept herself covered up when she had a sexy ass body. Her stomach wasn't as flat as Miki's, but it wasn't big either. Cyn had no reason to be self-conscious.

Bebe asked, "Ay, you think you could drop Kennedi off at school for me?"

"I'll be late," she called from the bathroom.

"But you'll be passing right by it."

"I won't have time to take her."

Sure, you won't, Bebe thought. He said, "You can't take her anyway. You're not on the list."

After bidding Cyn farewell Bebe got himself ready then went to get Kennedi ready. Arriving at the school Bebe didn't see Miki's truck. He was hoping to run into her. He may even sit in the parking lot to wait for her arrival if she hadn't been there already.

After signing Kennedi in he saw that Téa hadn't arrived yet. As he headed out the door he bumped right into Miki. She looked up and realized it was him. Her expression was of surprise mixed with somberness. After their gazes locked for a brief second Miki continued inside the classroom with Téa.

Bebe waited outside the classroom for her. She glanced at him and acted as if she didn't know why he was waiting. He fell in stride beside her. "How have you been?" he asked.

"Okay, I guess," she said dryly. She looked at him and asked, "How about you?"

"I'm good."

"Well it's nice seeing you and to actually hear your voice," she said but her face remained blank.

"Same here."

"Redd's out there so I gotta get back."

"Miki," he said softly. She turned to him then glanced down the corridor at the double doors. Bebe said, "I miss you."

Miki blinked back tears and nodded her acknowledgment of his statement. She continued to walk on in a dismal nature. Bebe could see that the shine from her personality had disappeared. She had returned to the same scared miserable person he met back in August. He had to remind himself that being apart from her was best.

Chapter 18

Bless looked at Sharif's innocent eyes. "Boy, I could be your baby auntie."

He smiled. "Man, age ain't shit Bless. I could treat you better than any other nigga, young or old."

"Boy, you still live at home with your mama. And I bet you got a curfew. You still get whoopings too, don't you?"

"You play too much. So, is that all it take to be your man? I need my own place?"

Bebe asked, "Sharif, how old are you exactly?" Bebe was at his sister's house which had become one of the most popular spots due to her adjacent neighbors. Bless lived next door to a middle-aged woman with two sons and a daughter that kept a lot of company. Every time Bebe came over it was something going on. Sharif was the younger son. The older brother was Malik, and their sister was Anandi.

"I just turned twenty," he answered.

"Bless is thirty-three," Bebe pointed out. "You know Lil Marvin only eight years younger than you."

Sharif shrugged.

Trina laughed. "How come you don't go after someone young like Free?"

Sharif shot Trina a look because Sharif knew she was being facetious. Free was the neighborhood menace. She wreaked havoc everywhere she went. Sharif said, "Nah. I like who I like."

Bebe asked as an insult to Trina, "You don't like bald

headed bitches with flat asses?" They had a love/hate relationship. Brandi was Bless' friend.

Trina cut her eyes at Bebe as Bless snickered. She looked up and out into the street. "Uh-oh y'all. Here come Leonard."

Leonard's long and lanky frame approached Bless' porch with all of them sitting around. "How y'all doing this evening night?"

"We good baby. What about your fine sexy self," Trina said stroking Leonard's ego and making him blush.

"Aw, you know I'm straight," Leonard said. "Whatchall folks getting into?"

"Nothing," Bless said.

Leonard looked at Sharif. "Ay, lemme get a dime."

"I gotcha," Durt, Sharif's friend said. He was about to reach in his pocket, but Sharif stopped him.

"Take that nigga to the store or something. Don't be serving right from her porch. What's wrong with you?" Sharif said in a firm tone. He was protective of Bless and didn't want to risk her wellbeing. Bebe was glad Sharif said something because he was about to kick Leonard's and Durt's ass.

"A'ight," Durt said. "Come on Leonard. Let's go to the store. Y'all want anything back?"

Trina asked, "Can I just go with you?"

"C'mon," Durt mumbled.

Bebe watched them walk off. He told the others, "Check and make sure all your shit is on you. Y'all know Leonard slick with that stealing."

A red Pontiac G6 drove up recklessly, barely missing the

young boys in the circle playing a game of basketball. From the driver's side a female's voice barked, "Move out the goddamn way!"

One of the boys hollered back, "Shut'cho crazy ass up and slow the fuck down!"

The boys weren't resuming their game until the car was no longer moving. The car parked behind Bless' car. Free got out of the driver side and mugged all of the boys and sneered, "What the fuck y'all looking at?"

"You hoe," one of them said with a snicker.

"I'ma whoop your lil ass!" Free threatened. She turned to the others and walked her pretty ass up to the porch. "What's up y'all?"

"What's up Free," Bebe said eyeing her seductively. Everybody said Free was crazy but to Bebe crazy was looking good. Free wasn't what he usually went for, but her sexiness was undeniable. She was petite with delicate curves and smooth milky chocolate skin. She had chinky eyes that were sexy to Bebe. He still wasn't sure if all the shiny black hair was hers on her head. They said she had a few screws loose but Bebe thought she was a trip.

Free eyed Bebe returning the same obvious lust and seduction. "Hey."

Monique finally exited the car on the passenger's side and twitched her slender hips up the driveway to the next-door porch. "Hey y'all. Hey Bebe."

"Uhm, I'ma need you to move your car," Bebe said pointing to it for emphasis. "You can't be blocking me in."

"You ain't about to leave anyway," Monique said with a

smile. “So, relax and chill. Enjoy this crazy December weather while you can.”

Free added, “As a matter of fact, come holler at me before you leave Bebe.”

Bebe smiled knowingly. If he didn’t know any better Free was starting to notice him. He watched the two ladies disappear inside their duplex on the other side of Bless.

Bless laughed, “Bebe, don’t be getting any ideas.”

“Naw but she smiling and shit. Usually she be mean mugging,” Bebe said.

Sharif quipped, “That’s because she been taking her medicine.”

“Where your girlfriend?” Bless asked Bebe.

“I ain’t got no muhfuckin girlfriend,” Bebe replied.

“I thought she was the jealous type and didn’t want you out of her sight,” Bless teased.

Bebe knew Bless was talking about Cyn because Deja loved running her mouth.

“I’ma stop messing with you,” Bless said. “Have you talked to Miki?”

“Naw. I try to avoid seeing her at the school,” Bebe said. No matter how much he tried to occupy his time in the company of Stefani or Cyn he still couldn’t get Miki off his brain. He had seen her a few times over the past couple of weeks. He told Bless he tried avoiding running into Miki, but he always hoped that he would bump into her. The few times he had seen her Redd had been with her. Bebe was wondering what that was about. And she was looking sadder every time he saw her. He wanted to hold her. He wanted to make love to her again. Furthermore, he wanted to remove her from Redd's grasp.

Miki hated that she had to let Redd know she was pregnant. He suspected it especially after her stomach had started to get a significant curvature to it. He said he always pull out. Miki had to remind him that he didn't always pull out even though she knew for a fact around the time of conception he did. Redd didn't seem happy. He complained that that was seven kids for him.

It was almost Christmas and Miki was fifteen weeks along. She was still trying to work up enough nerve to leave. She was trying to devise a plan. Since it was the winter months Redd was home more often. He wanted her to be right under him. He was even riding with her to take Téa to school. A few times she had seen Bebe watching from his truck. She pretended as if he wasn't right there, but she noticed.

Miki placed more of Téa's clothes in a garbage bag. She was very careful in her selections. She had to make it look like they were clothes she was getting rid of.

"Why you giving away so much?" Redd asked. He was standing in Téa's bedroom doorway.

He actually scared Miki because she didn't know he was standing there. "You just scared the crap out of me."

Redd sneered, "Yo scary ass."

You got me that way, Miki thought.

"Who you giving this stuff to any damn way?"

"To the church," she lied. She didn't understand why he was still angry at her. She had merely pointed out the obvious when she told him he was about to go out of town with another bitch. Miki didn't even care. The sooner he was gone, the better.

"Well I'm about to go," he said.

"Bye," she mumbled.

"Why the fuck you got an attitude Miki?"

"I don't have one." Miki sat down on Téa's bed. A wave of nausea hit her. She was in her second trimester and thought the nausea was supposed to subside at some point.

Redd walked over. Miki cowered thinking he was going to hit her. Instead he grabbed her by her face and squeezed in her cheeks real hard. "I done told you about you and your little pissy ass attitudes."

Miki tried to pry his hand away but it seemed as if he got tighter. He spat, "Just cause you pregnant won't keep you from getting yo ass beat." He pushed her by her face.

She bucked up to him like she was going to hit him. His reaction was to strike her in her face. "Bitch! I don't know who the fuck you think you is but yo ass ain't' mothafuckin crazy. Act like you gon hit me again!"

Miki held her face. She was too angry to cry. She was so tired of this treatment. Why did she stay with him? She couldn't blame nobody but herself.

"Let me take my ass on before I hurt your pregnant ass," he said.

Angry tears fell silently from her lids. She sat there until she heard him leave. She got up and started loading her truck with the bags of clothes she was supposedly getting rid of. She went back in the house. She went to her bathroom to prepare for a shower, but her reflection caught her attention. Her face was already turning red.

Miki hated herself and her life. Ever since Bebe called things off she felt her life had taken a dip. She didn't find much of anything enjoyable anymore. But she chose Redd over Bebe. Why? She wanted to believe in Redd. She wanted him to do right by her because he loved her. She wanted to be there for him during his journey to change. The truth was Redd wasn't trying to change. He would always be Redd and do as much as she allowed him.

Miki knew her family was tired of her declaring she was tired and making it seem as if she was going to do something about it only to renege. She was tired of wanting something more only to find herself feeling hopeless and helpless. She was tired of being scared. She remembered Bebe saying something about her freedom. As long as Redd was free she would never be.

Bebe. She sure did miss his silly butt. Miki called Maddie.

"Hello?"

"Hey Maddie. What are you doing?"

"If you're calling to see what Téa is doing, for the fiftieth-time woman she's doing fine!"

Miki chuckled, "I wasn't calling for her. I was tryna see what you were doing so I can drop these clothes off at your house. Redd is gone. He just left."

"Oh. Yeah. You talking about your getaway clothes?"

"Yeah."

"Yeah. Girl, come on."

Miki gathered her purse and keys and headed out. Why

was it necessary for Redd to go out of town at night? Miki wouldn't wreck her brain trying to figure out his lies. That was his life. A life she wished she could be very far away from.

Maddie met her at the door to take the two garbage bags of clothes. Maddie asked, "Did he see you with these bags?"

"Yeah, but he so stupid. I told him I was giving them to the church."

"Well you be careful going home. You pregnant by yourself and it's night out."

"I wonder if Bebe's home?" Miki mentioned.

Maddie smiled. "What you wondering about him for?"

"I miss him," she said.

"Go by there. I'm about to get out of this cold though. You go on home," Maddie said running back to her front door.

Miki went in the direction of Bebe's house when she left. His truck was there but his front porch light was out. The whole house seemed dark like no one was there. Maybe he was gone with somebody. It was Friday, so he was probably at somebody's club or party. Or possibly at a girl's house.

Miki parked behind his truck anyway. She got out and went to his door. She rang the doorbell. No answer. She got back in her vehicle. As she was backing out two sets of headlights approached. She almost felt embarrassed being caught in his driveway as the first little white car pulled in beside Bebe's truck. The SUV pulled along the front yard.

Miki watched as Bebe got out of the passenger seat of the white car. The driver was Cyn. The back door opened, and it was Deja. Out of the SUV hopped out Dinky and another guy Miki wasn't familiar with. Bebe handed everything in his hands to Deja and gave her the keys to his house so they could go in. He made his way over to her driver side window. Miki let the window down.

"What's up?" he asked.

Miki didn't know what to say. "I...uh...was in the neighborhood and thought I would ride by. I saw your truck in the driveway and thought you were here."

"Well I'm here now."

"And you have company," she said. "I didn't mean to intrude."

"What did you come by for?"

Miki half shrugged. She looked towards his house that was now coming to life. "It doesn't even matter. You got your friends to tend to."

"A'ight then," he said. "It was nice of you to stop by though."

Miki stared at him and wished he wouldn't be so stubborn. He knew what she was there for. He could see the anguish on her face. He knew she was hurt by what she saw.

Bebe began to walk away. Miki continued to back out of the driveway. Damn, did he not want to see her? This was his chance to see her without Redd around. She had to remind herself that he was the one that called their love affair off so why would he be the one wanting to see her.

About five minutes of driving Miki's phone rang. She answered, "Hello?"

"Come back," said Bebe on the other end.

"You have company," Miki said.

"They're gone. They were going out, and I decided not to. So please come back."

The desperation was back in his voice that Miki had grown accustomed to. A desperation that was entwined with passion and love but masked with indifference. Miki turned back around and headed back to Bebe's house.

As soon as Miki walked through the door Bebe attacked her with passionate kisses. Miki returned the same passion and hunger. They tore at each other's clothes. Bebe fucked her right there against the front door. It was the most sensual intense ardent lovemaking Miki had ever experienced. Bebe whispered to her over and over, "I love you so much."

"I love you too," Miki managed to say. She moaned louder as her body moved up and down against the door. Bebe kissed and sucked on her neck with a hunger that drove Miki to the edge.

After Bebe was done he picked her up and carried her all the way to his bedroom. He laid her on his bed where he proceeded to remove the rest of her clothing. Admiring her body, he planted kisses everywhere until he came to her belly. Miki noticed he hesitated but didn't say anything. He continued to caress her body with his kisses.

He knelt down in front of her. He lifted one of her legs over his shoulder and buried his face in her pussy. Miki let out a long wailing moan as he showed her clit tongue loving. She rested her hands on his head. She whispered softly, "Feels so good..."

He grabbed her by her ass firmly and lifted her in the air. Miki gasped. She giggled quickly throwing her other leg over his shoulder to stabilize her balance. Bebe had her on his strong shoulders eating the fuck out of her pussy. He didn't let up until she locked up and was grasping at his head lost in an overwhelming orgasmic explosion.

Bebe eased her down onto his bed. With her juices still on his face he kissed her passionately and aggressively. "I miss you so much Miki."

"I miss you too," Miki whispered.

"I don't want to talk about the obvious right now," he said. "I just wanna hold you for now. Okay?"

Miki nodded. She let him wrap his arms around her. In that moment she didn't care about a Redd. She was back in the arms of her love.

Chapter 19

While the kids were away she and Bebe went to The Mall at Green Hills. Miki spent her own money but Bebe was insistent that he do it. She let him do some but he had a fit when he saw the price of the True Religion jeans she wanted. Bebe didn't understand the logic behind spending a couple of hundred dollars on one pair of jeans. However, it was what Miki wanted. He even broke down and got himself a pair.

With bags in their hands they were ready to leave but Bebe saw a jewelry store he wanted to go in and look around. He asked Miki, "What kind of ring you want?"

Miki smiled coyly as she looked at the sparkling gems in the case. "Whatchu talking about rings for?"

"Why do a couple look at rings?" he asked.

Miki half shrugged still wearing an uneasy smile. She asked, "So we're a couple now?"

"I'm not letting you go back."

A salesman came over. "Is there anything I can help you with?"

"We're looking at engagement rings," Bebe told him.

"Well my name is Josh and I'd be glad to be of assistance," Josh said.

There was one particular ring that caught Miki's eye, but she knew it was way over an expected amount from Bebe. He was tight and wasn't frivolous with his money. He didn't live to impress other people which was something Miki appreciated about him.

Miki pointed to that ring, “Can I see that one?”

Josh removed it from the case and handed it to Miki. She studied it, slipped it on her finger and admired how it looked.

Josh said, “That’s a nice one. The one you’re wearing is a one and half carat. It can come up to a five-carat.”

“That’s the one you like?” Bebe asked.

Still wearing the goofy smile, Miki nodded.

Bebe held his hand out for it. Miki was hesitant to give it to him because she knew he was going to look at the price. And he did just that. He pretended to choke. “Got damn. Are you serious?”

Miki chuckled with embarrassment and shook her head. Josh stood there grinning.

Bebe said, “I’d be forever paying on that. How long is y’all layaway?”

More embarrassed Miki started to inch away and look at more rings.

Josh said, “I can have her sized and we can get that back in about four days. Do you have an account with us or would you like to get one?”

“My credit fucked up,” Bebe said. “If I can’t do layaway or pay cash it ain’t happening.”

Oh my God, Miki thought. As embarrassing as it was, it was still humorous. She was tickled.

“Now that lady looked like she fell in love with that ring. You gotta get it for her,” Josh said. “And we have a nice paved diamond bridal band that would go nicely with that.”

"How much is that?"

"It would be an additional fifteen hundred," Josh said grabbing the finger measuring rings.

"Damn, you tryna bust a nigga head," Bebe groaned.

Miki shook her head and was ready to walk out of the jewelry store. Josh asked to see her hand. She said, "Oh no. we're not getting anything. You hear him, don't you."

"Before he leaves here he's getting something," Josh said matter of factly as he slid a couple of rings over her finger.

Bebe said, "Bae, how 'bout you apply for the credit and I'll make the payments on it."

Was he serious? Miki giggled and flushed. She said, "You know what? I'm about to go across the way to Juicy Couture."

Bebe chuckled sneakily. He winked at Josh. He said to Miki, "But wait. Don't you want the ring?"

Miki shook her head as she walked out of the store. Bebe told Josh, "I wanted her to leave. I knew she would."

"What do you have up your sleeve?" Josh asked suspiciously.

"I want that ring in a three-carat with the bridal ring," Bebe said as he pulled out his wallet.

"Three?" Josh asked with a raised eyebrow.

Bebe nodded. He pulled out a credit card. Josh gave him a shaming look. "You're full of trickery."

"Yeah, I want her to think I'm tight with my money," he laughed.

Josh was thrilled. "Oh, I love this. You're gonna have to come back in here and tell me how she reacts when you give it to her."

Bebe wasn't sure if he was going to present it to Miki right away. He would just hold on to the ring and when the time was right he would propose. Right now, he was trying to fill her out and see where her head was.

The next morning, they were awakened by the violent ringing of the doorbell and banging on the door. It startled Miki. She immediately panicked. "Redd knows I'm here."

Bebe threw his pajama bottoms on and he grabbed a t-shirt. "Even if he did you're here now. What can he do? But that's not him. I know who this is."

Bebe didn't have to ask who it was. He opened the door and in walked Stefani. "I thought you were bringing BJ back last night."

"I was tired. What do you want?" he asked.

"I need two hundred dollars. My phone cut off," she said. "I woulda called you but I couldn't."

Bebe sighed. "I don't have it."

"Yeah you do. I know you do."

"Work is slowing down. You know how I am when the winter months get here. I ain't got money to be spending like that."

Stefani looked Bebe up and down. Her eyes lingered on his dick print. She could tell he wasn't wearing any underwear. She smiled wickedly as she neared him. "Your dick hard ain't it?"

"Yeah and I was about to take care of it before you came

here to get on my nerves," he said.

"How you plan to take care of it?" she asked. She said, "I can help you out with it."

"That's all right. My girl got me," he said with a smirk.

"Your girl? What girl?"

"Don't worry about all that. I got BJ. He got clothes and shit over here."

Stefani frowned. She wanted to know who this girl was. Seeing the expression on her face Bebe said, "You'll meet her soon enough."

"I ain't worry about your lil girlfriend. I just need the two hundred."

"Let me look into some stuff and I'll get back with you."

"How? I don't have a phone."

"Oh. My bad. I call you on your job or you just call me back by six."

"This some bullshit," she grumbled.

"You got your nerves. You the one that let your shit get cut off. I need you to leave now cause you really blocking."

Stefani rolled her eyes. She knew she would get the two hundred but on Bebe's time. "Tell your little girlfriend your baby mama said hey."

Bebe couldn't wait to close the door on her. He looked at the time on his kitchen stove as he walked by. He and Miki had thirty minutes to get it in before having to get the kids ready.

He hurried up and stripped back to nakedness and snuggled behind Miki. She asked without turning around, "Who was that?"

“BJ mama,” he said.

“Pocahontas?”

“Yep,” he said as he started poking her from behind.

Miki giggled. “Boy, if you ain’t crazy.”

“Go on and poke your ass out and let me get up in this,” he said squeezing her hip.

“We gotta get the kids ready,” she said.

“They straight,” he said easing inside her. She let a moan escape her lips. He pumped in and out of her in such a sensual way. He held onto her and she held onto his arms. The way he made Miki felt was nothing like Redd had made her feel. Sex with Bebe was loving, fun, and exciting. And she couldn’t believe he was actually making love to her without protection.

They were so caught up in their lovemaking that they didn’t realize Kennedi had walked in. “Daddy!”

“Shit! Kennedi get out,” Bebe hissed looking back at his daughter.

Miki started giggling. She asked, “How come you didn’t lock the door?”

“I never do,” he said under his breath.

“Shadow and me want some cerio with flarshflallows,” Kennedi said.

“I’ll be in there in a minute,” Bebe said.

“Hurry up!” Kennedi demanded as she walked out of the room.

Miki cracked up. Bebe said, “That shit ain’t funny. And what the hell is some flarshflallows?”

Later, after Bebe left the house, Miki decided it would be a good time to call her friend and get caught up.

Kat asked, "Where are you now?"

"I'm with Bebe."

"Mmm hmm. That's what I thought," Kat said. "So, what are your plans?"

"I wish I didn't have to go back. But I'm leaving. I've been taking my stuff over Maddie's house pretending they were clothes we giving away to the church."

"You're serious huh?"

"As a heart attack."

"Are you doing this because of good dick?" Kat laughed.

Miki said, "Not because of that. I mean that part is good but Bebe was getting tired and I don't think I'm willing to lose him. He's good to me."

"Where is he now?"

"He went somewhere. I'm here with the kids."

"I would come over there, but I'll probably be followed," Kat joked.

"I know."

There was a knock on the door and the doorbell sounded. Miki said, "Hold on Kat. Somebody at his door."

Miki went to the window to look out first. It was two women. She opened the door. It was Pocahontas and some other chick.

Stefani looked Miki up and down. "Where's Bebe?"

"He's not here," Miki said.

"Where did he go?" Stefani asked.

"I don't know. He just left."

"And he left you here with our kids?" she sneered.

Miki was annoyed. She said, "I'll have him to call you when he gets back."

"I'll just wait," Stefani said welcoming herself in. She was followed by her friend. The friend looked at Miki real hard.

Stefani went towards the rec room where the kids were playing leaving her friend behind. The friend kept staring at Miki. Miki asked, "Can I help you?"

"Aren't you Redd's baby mama?" she asked.

Miki studied the girl and suddenly realized who she was. Her name was Karmen and she was Raquel's sister. Raquel was Redd's wife. Kat asked, "Who is that bitch that know you?"

Miki said, "You're Karmen right?"

"Yeah. I didn't know you and Redd weren't together no more," Karmen said.

Miki said nothing. Damn! She didn't want her going back running her mouth to her sister. Raquel wouldn't hesitate to tell Redd of Miki's whereabouts.

Stefani came back into the living room going into the kitchen. She grabbed the cordless landline phone. "I'm calling Bebe real quick."

Karmen asked, "So you got tired of Redd's shit too?"

Miki said, "Why you say that?"

"I mean I wouldn't blame you. I be telling my sister she

need to go ahead and divorce his ass. And Alicia and Tamika are stupid. You was but I see you done moved on...With Stefani's man," Karmen laughed throwing shade towards Stefani.

"He and I are just friends," Miki said.

"Sure, you are," Karmen said with doubt. She looked at the relaxed way Miki was dressed. *Just friends my ass*, she thought.

Stefani could be heard fussing with Bebe. "Yeah I'm in your house...Why you got her watching our kids? How you gon leave her up in your house like that?...Cause...he's my son too...I don't care...How long?...Whatever...And you gon be calling me with some slick shit wanting me over here...Whatever Bebe...I'll believe it when I see it...Where's my two hundred dollars?"

Miki made up her mind that she didn't like Stefani and wasn't sure if she could deal with her. Miki went into Bebe's bedroom. "Girl you hear them?"

"You know she's running to Raquel, right?" Kat asked.

"I know. I really don't care," Miki said. It was too late for regrets or consequences. She had made her move.

Miki's line beeped. It was Redd. "Kat this is Redd. I'ma see where his head at."

"Okay and call me right back."

Miki took his call. "Hello?"

His voice was calm and really low. "What are you doing?"

"Nothing." She answered with the same tone.

"I was just calling to let you know that I'ma be running

later than what I thought. I probably won't be back until in the morning," he said.

Miki wasn't sure if this was a setup or what. But it was Sunday and he usually never stayed gone past Sunday. For all she knew he could be home trying to trick her. Miki said, "Okay."

"I'll see you tomorrow. Tell Téa I love her."

"Okay. Bye."

"Wait. How you feeling?"

"I'm good."

"Okay. Bye love."

Miki rolled her eyes as the call ended. She laid in Bebe's bed and thought of how wonderful he was. If he extended the offer for her to stay again she might just have to take it. Miki was tired of being tired of Redd. She despised him and no longer respected him. She hoped the baby she carried was not his.

"Miki?"

Miki's eyes opened wide. She had fallen asleep and didn't realize Bebe had come back to the house. He was hovering over her looking down into her eyes. For a minute she thought it was Redd hollering at her. "You scared the shit out of me."

"Sorry. Are you hungry?"

"A little," she said.

Bebe rubbed her stomach. "You know we gotta talk about this."

"I know," she mumbled.

"Are you pregnant?"

"Why you ask that?"

"I know your body. Your stomach don't round out like this. And you're tired. You get exhausted by lifting one leg. And your pussy feel different."

Miki rolled her eyes playfully. "So that's what you mean when you said we gotta talk about this? I thought you were talking about us."

"That too. But I wanna know how far along you are."

"Fifteen weeks."

"How come you didn't tell me sooner?"

"I didn't want to keep you by saying I'm pregnant. Besides I don't know whose it is."

"It's mine."

Miki laughed. "How can you be sure?"

"I just know. I can feel it. And it happened in the club didn't it?"

Miki grinned. He was something else. She said, "If you are the father then yeah it did."

"Does he know you're pregnant?"

"Yeah. I had to break down and tell him. He doesn't care one way or the other."

Bebe laid on his back. "Well, you know I'ma need you to make a different choice Miki."

"That was another reason why I didn't tell you," Miki said.

"I figured that too. But I'ma still need you to make a choice baby. I can't have you over there pregnant with my child and he hitting on you and shit."

“You still wanna be with me like that?”

“Why wouldn’t I? I was just doing what I thought was the smart thing for me to do. How do you think it made me feel to spend that lil bit of time with you only for you to return to him? That shit wasn’t feeling good.”

“I’m sorry. But if it makes you feel any better know that I’ve been taking my clothes to Maddie’s a little bit at a time. I’ve already taken a few personal items too. I got so much shit he doesn’t even notice.”

“That’s nice to know. So, when are you leaving?”

“I was thinking when I go to my mama’s for Christmas that I was going to tell him I’m not returning.”

“That’s in three days.”

“Yeah. What time is it?” she asked.

“It’s almost four.”

“I gotta go get Téa and get back to the house like everything is okay,” she said. “There’s a few more things I need to pack.”

“I don’t want you to go,” he whined.

“Hopefully next weekend we won’t have this problem.”

“So, you say.”

Miki smiled softly. “I know we won’t.”

Chapter 20

About an hour after Miki departed from his presence, Bebe received a call. It was an urgent call. His mother was hysterical and crying. She was able to manage the words, "Vanderbilt...your sister."

The first thought was something happened to Bless. Bebe pushed all other thoughts out his mind. All he could focus on was his sister. He and the kids dressed and headed for Vanderbilt.

Marvin had gone to Bless' place claiming to want to see the boys. Again, he cornered Bless in the kitchen. Lil Marvin explained that they started talking louder and arguing. Next thing he knew his mother was screaming. Lil Marvin described seeing his father stab his mother multiple times. Fearing his and Marcus' life they fled the house and went next door to Trina's. Trina called 9-1-1. Marvin left before the police got there. Bless was rushed to the hospital.

"I'm killing him Mama," Bless said with anger and determination. It was a matter of fact that Bebe was killing Marvin.

"No," Joyce said firmly. "Let the police do their job. He'll get his."

"He's still out there. They ain't doing their gotdamn jobs!" Bebe said, his voice rose. The other people in the emergency room waiting area looked over at them.

Deja tried to console him by rubbing his back. "Calm down Bebe."

Bebe shrugged her off of him. He got up and headed

outside. He didn't smoke but this would be a good time to start. Cyn was hurrying from the parking lot. He called Cyn's name. She walked over. "What happened Bebe!"

"She's fine. He didn't hit anything major," Bebe said somberly. "They're stitching her up. He punctured her thirteen times though."

Cyn looked on in disbelief. Bebe said, "She's gonna be okay. All I know is he ain't gonna be once I find his ass and kill him."

"No Bebe," Cyn cried. "If you kill him then we won't have you anymore."

Bebe knew that was the rational way but he wasn't feeling very sensible at the moment. Shit like this was what he was afraid of for Miki.

Shortly after Free, Trina, Sharif and Monique all showed up at the hospital concerned about Bless.

"Let's go beat that nigga's ass, Bebe," Free said to him. They were in the family room waiting area.

"Don't encourage him," Monique said. "Please."

Bebe didn't reply. He thanked God that his sister was okay. If something else had happened to her he wouldn't know what he would have done. However his mind was on Miki. Redd was just as crazy if not crazier than Marvin. No one knew Marvin was capable of going to these lengths. There was no telling what Redd was capable of doing. Miki might not be as fortunate as Bless. And Miki was carrying his child. No, she had to get away from Redd right away.

Bebe pulled out his phone and sent Miki a text: call me asap!

Cyn walked back into the waiting room. She looked over at Bebe and wondered who he was texting with. She sat down beside him. “Hey.”

“Hey,” he mumbled not looking away from his phone.

“I hadn’t seen or talked to you since Friday. You okay?” she asked.

“I was until this shit,” he said.

“Bless is fine. She’s in there talking and in good spirits,” Cyn said in a comforting manner. She caught Free cutting her eyes at her. Cyn frowned with disapproval. She asked Bebe, “You and her got something going on or something?”

“Who?” he asked finally looking up at her.

She nodded towards Free.

Bebe actually smiled. “Naw. She just crazy.”

Cyn ignored Free. She asked Bebe, “So did you and ol’ girl talk Friday?”

“What makes you think that?” he mused.

“Because she showed up at your house and you started acting weird. Then you didn’t even wanna go out with us. I assume you must’ve called her back.”

“We did talk,” he said. His phone alerted him to a received text. Beautiful: can’t talk right now, will call later

“Oh yeah,” Cyn stated.

Bebe looked over at Cyn. “I guess I need to tell you this. I ain’t tryna lead you on or nothing and I’m sorry if you thought me and you could have anything more. But I’ma try to make things work with Miki.”

Cyn was displeased. She rolled her eyes and exhaled

heavily. "I figure that."

"She's pregnant and we're going to be together."

"Really? How you know it isn't her man's baby?"

Bebe looked at her wondering how much Deja had ran her mouth about. Bebe replied, "That would be my concern and not yours."

"Don't be stupid Bebe."

"Not being stupid would mean you and I continue to see each other?" he questioned.

"I'm not saying that."

"Look, I enjoyed our little time together, but it was just that. Miki has my heart."

Cyn didn't have a reply. Her eyebrows furrowed as she sat in deep thought.

"I'm sorry," Bebe said softly.

Cyn half shrugged. "I'm fine. Just hope you're fine."

Miki sat in her truck and let her mind wander. How could she get away from Redd for good? He would have to spend some time in prison to allow her enough time to move far away and get settled into a new life. She had an aunt that lived in Virginia. She could go there and start an entirely brand-new life. She knew Redd wouldn't allow her to leave just like that. Miki needed to devise a plan.

Instead of going home Miki went to Kat's. When Miki got there, she was surprised to see Kat with a purple bruise on her neck. "What happened?"

"Whatchu think?" Kat said incredulously.

"I thought you said Ox wasn't trippin' like that," Miki said sitting on the couch. "Did he choke you or something?"

Kat started laughing. "Girl these ain't those kind of bruises. This come from someone sucking on my neck."

"Ox?"

Kat gave an evasive shrug with a sneaky grin.

Miki gasped in surprise. "Kat! How did you explain that Ox?"

"I didn't," Kat said. She snickered, "The nigga think he did it."

Miki shook her head shaming her friend. Kat sat down beside Miki. She said, "I'm thinking about leaving."

"Leaving Ox?"

"Yeah. But not just him. I'm thinking about leaving Tennessee."

"No Kat. You can't leave me. You're the only friend I have," Miki said with feigned sadness.

"You're crazy. You have Maddie and Kizzie."

"Yeah but they're boring," Miki said. "Where are you going?"

"Atlanta."

"Atlanta!" Miki exclaimed. "Everybody going to Atlanta."

"Dwayne's family live there."

Miki's mouth dropped open in shock. "You leaving with him?"

Kat nodded. She quickly said, "Well I haven't confirmed it yet."

"What is Ox gon do?"

"Don't even care," Kat said. "I'm so sick of his shit. Him and that bitch can have each other."

"Well I'm leaving after Christmas," Miki said matter of factly.

"I can't wait to see how Redd will react to that. What is Bebe saying?"

"You know he's happy I'm leaving. Especially after I told him about the baby."

"So, you told him you were pregnant?"

"Yep. He believes the baby is his. I do too but I can't be one hundred percent sure."

"Wow. I guess you and I both are overdue for change."

"Yep," Miki said looking down at her phone. A text was received. Redd: where r u?

Miki: Kat's y

Redd: cum home u been gone long enuff

Miki: I'm on my way'

Miki sighed. "Well that's him. He wants me home. I guess I talk with you later."

"Okay. And be careful," Kat said.

Once inside her truck Miki called Bebe.

He answered, "Hello?"

"Hey Elmo!"

"Elmo my ass. Don't call me that shit."

Miki giggled. Because Bebe was so ticklish Miki started calling him by the popular kid's toy's name.

"Ay, there's something I need to tell you," Bebe said. His tone had changed to a somber one.

"What is it?" Miki asked.

"My sister was stabbed by her husband," Bebe said. "I'm worried about you and I don't want you to end up like her. Especially with you carrying my baby. So, if I gotta come over there and get you myself, I will."

"Is she okay?" Miki's heart had dropped at hearing the news. "I can't believe it. Oh my God. Is she all right, Bebe?"

"She's okay. She's stitched up," he said.

"When did this happen?"

"Right after you left."

"Is that why you wanted to talk to me?"

"Yep. Come on, Miki."

"Come on what?"

"You know. Come home to me baby. Don't even go back to the house with him."

"I'm leaving Bebe. Right after Christmas."

"That's too long."

"Two days Bebe."

"Do you know what he could do to you in those two days?"

"There's more stuff I need to get," she explained.

"I'll replace it," he said.

"Bebe." She said his name with frustration. She hated when he put her on the spot.

"Mikina," he countered.

It made Miki smile when he used her birth name. She liked the way it sound rolling off his lips. "If he's there I will stay. If he's not, I'll go ahead and grab the things I need and come over to your house."

"Baby, forget that stuff."

"Bebe, don't do that. I'll be there, okay."

He exhaled impatiently and groaned. "Okay. But if you're not here by Christmas Day I'm coming to get you."

Miki shook her head at his insistence. They spoke a few minutes more until Miki pulled up to her house. Redd wasn't there so she needed to move as fast as she could.

Miki went from room to room gathering things. She felt like Celie from The Color Purple when she was trying to leave with Shug.

"What are you doing?"

Miki nearly jumped out of her skin. She stammered, "N-n-nothing."

Redd looked at the clothes and shoes Miki had pulled out of the closet. "That look like most of your shit, Miki. I know you ain't doing what it looks like you're doing."

Miki giggled nervously, "What's that, Redd?"

"Leaving me. Is that what you're doing?" he asked with his head cocked to the side.

"No. I'm just going through this stuff to see what else I want to depart with. This is the season for giving, you know.

You need to go through some of your stuff too."

"I wear all of my shit," he said.

Miki was relieved that he was falling for it.

"We going out tonight to Demon Knights' Christmas party," he said.

"On a Monday? Who has a party on a Monday night?"

"The bike clubs do. It's their regular bike night anyway."

"I don't feel like going out," Miki called out to him as he went into the closet.

"Why not?"

"I'm pregnant and I'm sick," she said. "I don't feel too good."

"You'll be alright. Go on and call your mama."

Miki sighed. She called Ava. When she answered Miki said, "Hey Mama."

"Hey babycakes," Ava chirped.

"What are you and Larry doing?"

"Nothing. Just sitting here. Why?"

"Can you watch your grandchild and her sister one more night?"

"You must be going out. With who?"

"Redd."

"What happened to Bebe?"

"Mama, you know I can't talk about that, right?"

"He don't have to know what you're talking about. So, what happened to Bebe? You don't talk about him as much."

"Still there."

Ava scoffed. "I think he's stupid too."

"Too?" Miki asked incredulously. She laughed. "What are you trying to say?"

"Both of you are stupid. You sit there with that man who doesn't make you happy. And he sitting right there being your side piece waiting on you to come to your senses."

"Whatever, Mama. Will you watch them?"

"I guess. They already here. But will you be getting them tomorrow at least?"

"Yep."

"Okay. Bring them on."

Miki told Redd she had the girl's taken care of. He was already dressing for a night out. Miki decided with a loose-fitting blouse with a pair of relaxed cut jeans. Her days of wearing skin tight clothing was over.

"Baby, you couldn't dress sexier than that?" Redd asked.

Miki looked down at herself. She thought she looked okay. "I told you I wasn't feeling too good. Can I at least be comfortable?"

"Yeah, I guess."

Redd took her to a bike club party. It was also a birthday bash for one of Demon Knights' leading men. Going to their usual sitting area Miki was glad to be meeting up with Mokeba, Kat, Kim and Toya.

"What's up girl?" Mokeba greeted.

"Hey y'all," Miki replied as she sat down.

"Miki, you don't look too good," Toya commented. "Where's your makeup?"

"She all naked face," Kim added.

"I don't feel good. I didn't feel like coming to this shit," Miki said.

Kat gave Miki and sympathetic look. "That baby sick."

Miki shot Kat a look. Kat grinned. She leaned closer to Miki so that she could only hear, "Girl, I'm about to do some of you and Bebe's shit."

"What are you talking about?" Miki asked.

"The restroom," Kat laughed.

"With who?" Miki asked.

Kat's eyes traveled to Toya.

Miki shook her head to shame Kat. "Shame on you girl." Miki looked around and observed Dwayne talking right in front of Ox's face. Damn shame. At least her side piece wasn't a part of the group.

"So how you been Miki?" Mokeba asked.

"Good," Miki said. She noticed the way Mokeba was grinning at her. "What?"

"I heard something about you," she said.

Miki cut her eyes at Kat assuming she ran her mouth about her pregnancy. "What you hear?"

"You got you a little piece on the side," Mokeba said.

Miki glanced Redd's way to make sure he wasn't close by to be hearing any of this. "Be quiet. You tryna get my head chopped."

Mokeba laughed. “Girl he ain’t thinking about us.”

“Shit. He got radar ears,” Miki said. She asked, “So what are you talking about? A side piece?”

Kat said, “Yeah. What are you talking about?”

“Somebody said that Keonte’s cousin got the hots for you,” Mokeba said.

“Keonte? Who is Keonte?” Miki asked with genuine confusion.

“Don’t be playing dumb,” Toya teased.

“I don’t know who that is. For real,” Miki said.

Kim said, “There they go right there.” She nodded her head in the direction of a group of men moving through the crowd.

Miki looked, and her heart began beating wildly. Bebe was there. Miki forgot that Bebe had a cousin that belonged to one of the bike clubs. There he was looking gorgeous in his all-black attire. Miki watched him interact with the men around him. He was clowning around. A smile crept across Miki’s face.

“It must be true,” Mokeba teased. “Look at that smile on your face.”

“No. They just being silly, and I was reacting to it,” Miki countered. She wouldn’t admit nothing to them. The only person Miki trusted was Kat.

“Sure, you were,” Toya said.

Miki watched as woman after woman made their way to Bebe. Bebe was definitely hot with the ladies. Miki wanted to see him desperately, but if she got up and went his way now it would look very suspicious.

"I know he look good though," Kim said.

"Y'all stop looking," Kat said. "Redd an'nem looking over here."

Miki glanced back at Redd and he was staring right at her. He motioned for her to come to him. "Here we go," she said under her breath.

"Yes," she said when she walked up to Redd.

He turned his back to his boys and talked to her. "What are you doing?"

"Sitting over there with the ladies," she answered with confusion.

"Who you looking at?"

"Mokeba and Toya were saying something about somebody out there."

"Are you sure it wasn't that nigga?"

"What nigga?"

"Don't play dumb with me."

"I don't know what you're talking about, Redd," she said.

"I tell you what. I'll give you a few hours to think about it and when I ask you again you can either tell me or you can get your ass kicked," he said calmly.

"I don't know what—"

She was interrupted by Redd grabbing her face hard and squeezing her jaws. "Shut up sometimes, Miki." He released her.

Miki frowned, too mad to be embarrassed. "Why are you doing me like that?"

“I’ve heard some shit, Miki,” he said.

The look in his eyes let Miki know he knew the truth. She looked away, “Can I go back to the table?” She saw Karmen with Pocahontas looking her way. Pocahontas was smirking. Karmen waved. She said, “Hey Miki. Hey Redd.”

Redd said, “What’s up.”

Miki’s frown deepened. She knew Karmen went back running her mouth. How else would Redd know?

Redd said, “Keep your eyes at the mothafuckin table. If I catch you looking in that nigga’s direction I will bust you in both of your goddamn eyes. You hear me?”

Miki went back to table fuming. She dared not to look up. She didn’t want to face their questioning eyes.

“What he say?” Kat asked.

“I don’t even wanna talk about it,” Miki mumbled.

“I ain’t gon lie,” Toya said. “Dwayne told me that Redd told him you were fucking around.”

Kat was taken aback. “Dwayne need to shut up.”

“Dwayne didn’t say it, Redd did,” Toya defended.

“I know. But he don’t need to be spreading other people’s shit that may or may not be true,” Kat snapped.

“It’s just me though,” Toya said.

“Yeah, and you told Mokeba and Kim. That’s where Mokeba got that ‘I heard something about you’ from.”

“Well damn Kat, you act like it’s you we talking about,” Mokeba said.

“All I’m saying is none of them niggas over there can’t talk about nobody's shit when they be doing the most especially Dwayne." Kat was upset.

Miki pat Kat on the thigh. "I'm okay Kat." Only Miki understood where Kat's anger was coming from. But now Miki wondered how Redd assumed she was seeing somebody. And he was specific because he knew who Miki was looking at.

"Uh-oh," Kim said under her breath. Miki looked up to see what Kim was talking about. Bebe and a few of his people were making their way to where they were. Miki looked away and tried to focus on Kat's shoes. She could feel Bebe's eyes on her. She could even hear his silent pleas. "Miki, look at me baby." But she couldn't. She was immobilized by the feel of Redd's stare.

Kat said to Miki, "Bebe's crazy."

"Why you say that?" Miki asked looking only at Kat's face.

"He just is. He waved to me," Kat said. "He mean-mugged the hell out of Redd though."

Miki rolled her eyes and sighed. "Why did he do that?"

"I told you he crazy."

Chapter 21

It was now Tuesday morning and Miki awakened to a sore and aching body. She went to get out of the bed and was stopped by the rope tied to the railing of the bed. The other end was knotted around her left wrist. Redd had snapped on her Saturday night. He beat on her throughout the whole day on Sunday. He let her rest Monday. She wanted to forget that it happened.

Redd accused her of fucking around with Bebe specifically. He knew Bebe's name. He knew what type of work he was in. He knew he had a daughter the same age as Téa and she went to the same school as Téa.

"So, all this time you've been fucking him, haven't you, Miki?" Redd had asked.

Miki was already terrified and feared for her life. She had been cornered in between the bed and the nightstand. She was cowered on the floor ready to protect herself by balling up. He had already punched her in the face several times. Her left eye felt like it was scratched, and it ached. She was tasting blood. There was a throbbing pain emitting from her left arm. She had backed up in between the nightstand and the bed to shield herself.

"Bitch, I oughta kick your pussy in," he snarled kicking her legs.

Miki drew her legs up to protect her stomach. If he knew she was pregnant with Bebe's child, he would surely make her lose it intentionally.

"Get up!"

“Please Redd!” Miki cried. “Please, please, please! Whatever you think I did, I’m sorry.”

“No. It’s what I know,” Redd said. “You so fucking dumb. I just got tired of letting you get away with the shit. Montiece told me about your stupid ass. Then Raquel told me that you was at that nigga house like you fucking lived there. How long you been fucking him Miki?”

“I haven’t been fucking nobody,” she said.

Redd reached down and jerked Miki out from in between the nightstand and the bed. Miki tore away from his grasp and made a run for the bathroom. She managed to get the door locked. She went straight for the bathroom window. She tried to open it, but it wouldn’t budge. The locks. She unlocked it as Redd kicked in the bathroom door. She tried to hoist herself up but was stopped by the lashing of his belt against her back. It stung enough to cause her to fall down. Like a runaway slave Redd beat her across the back, arms, and legs with that belt. He shouted, spit, and fumed while throwing out insults at her.

When he got tired and only when he got tired he allowed her to get in the bed where he proceeded to tie her to the bed, so she couldn’t get away. The beating had exhausted her. Even if he hadn’t tied her up Miki wasn’t going anywhere.

“I need to pee,” she said. Her lips felt heavy and they hurt.

There was no response.

She yelled, “Redd!”

Seconds later he appeared in the doorway of the bedroom. Miki said, “I gotta pee.”

“Hold it,” he said and walked away.

He returned several minutes later willing to allow her to

relieve herself.

After she was done, he followed her back to the bed. This time he didn't bother to tie her back up. He sat on the edge of the bed looking at her. There was anger still in his eyes. He pulled out Miki's phone. "What's his number?"

Miki didn't want to tell him.

"I'ma ask you again. Which one is his number?"

"I don't have his number," Miki said sticking to her lie.

"Miki, do you need me to do what I did last night?"

Miki started to cry. "No."

"I had you followed, Miki. I know where this nigga live and everything. He got a house on Kenwood right around the fuckin corner from your sister. So, you might as well come clean about it."

When Miki still didn't say anything, Redd balled up his fist and went to strike her. She yelled, "Okay! Please don't hit me. It's Ms. Brenda."

"I had a feeling it was, but I wasn't sure 'cause I talked to that lady."

Miki watched him tap the screen then tapped it again. She heard the ringtone signifying that he had the phone on speaker.

"Hello?" Bebe answered.

Redd motioned to her to speak as he held the phone close to her. Miki said, "Hey."

"You okay?" Bebe asked.

Redd nodded his head at her. She said, "Yeah."

"Will I see you today?"

"No."

"Baby, what's wrong? Did he do something to you?"

Miki didn't reply.

Bebe got quiet. Miki knew Bebe wasn't stupid. He asked, "You didn't call me, did you?"

Miki didn't say anything. She just looked at Redd.

Bebe said, "Where that punk ass nigga?"

"I'm right here nigga," Redd stated. "What's up?"

"What's up? You called me."

"Miki called you. Her number showed up in your phone, not mine."

This was going to be a disaster, Miki thought. She knew Bebe wasn't the type that took well to threats. Bebe had been wanting to get to Redd for some time now.

"What's up with you and my lady? What she need to see you today for? Y'all fucking?"

"Miki is my friend. You can think whatever you wanna think about what we do. That's on you my nigga."

"What the fuck that mean?"

"It means what the fuck I said. You can think whatever you wanna think."

"You needa stay away from mine. Ya feel me?"

"Naw my nigga. I don't feel nothing 'bout whatchu sayin'."

"So whatchu tryna say?"

"You can't tell me what the fuck I need to do. Whatchu

needa do is keep yo mothafuckin hands off Miki. You wanna lay hands on somebody then fight me nigga."

"Well what then nigga? Bring your ass over here! Cause after I kick your ass I'ma beat this bitch's ass. Both of y'all will be some busted up muhfuckas fucking with me."

"My nigga...you shouldn't have invited me over. And when I get there, and she look like she's been touched by you, I'ma fuck you up."

Miki's mind floated somewhere else as the two men went back and forward. Miki knew that when Redd got off that phone, he would take everything out on her. She wanted to run. She hoped someone, anyone would come by to prevent him from killing her. Knowing him he probably wouldn't let anybody in the house to see her bruised.

Redd ended the call on Bebe. He had enough of Bebe's arrogance and his threats. "So, you think this nigga give a shit about you? I guess you in love and shit. You wanna leave me for him, Miki? Fuck that nigga! Fuck a Bebe! You want his ass?"

Miki shook her head. "We just friends. It ain't nothing between us like that."

Redd backhanded her. "Bitch, stop lying!"

Miki started crying again. She could taste fresh blood. She drew her knees up into her chest preparing for him to beat on her. He glared at her. "You out here fucking around got me looking stupid and shit. Bitch, I oughta slice your damn throat."

Miki's pitiful expression seemed to anger Redd even more. He drew his arm back as if he was about to hit her. Miki cowered ready to block the blow.

Instead of hitting her, a crazed expression covered Redd's face. He hopped up from the bed abruptly and said venomously, "Bitch, I'm just gonna kill yo' ass."

Miki believed that he actually would this time. Frightened, her eyes followed him until he disappeared in the walk-in closet. He was going for his gun. He wouldn't find it because Miki had moved it which would only anger him even more. Miki's heart began thumping profoundly in her chest. Why hadn't she listened? Why did she have to be so hard headed?

A shine caught her eye and she looked down on the bed before her. It was her set of keys that apparently had fallen from Redd's pockets. This was it. It was an opportunity she knew she had to take. While he was cursing and searching in the closet, Miki reached over and covered the keys with her hand. Carefully she closed her fingers around them, so they wouldn't make any noises.

Terrified, knowing that her chances of getting away were slim and her suffering a harsher punishment, Miki stood to her feet. Quietly she eased toward the bedroom door. She had to take this chance.

Once she felt sure, she quickly stepped into the hallway and pulled the door closed to provide some difficulties for him when he came for her.

Miki bolted down the stairs despite the pain her body had endured. When she made it to the bottom of the stairs she could hear his angry footsteps. With no time to look back she made a dash for the front door. In her plight to flee she didn't bother shutting the door behind her. With just socks on her feet, pajama shorts and the matching top Miki ran for her car.

By the time she jumped in the driver's seat, Redd was

jumping from the front porch, just a few feet away from the driveway and her vehicle.

Instinct made her lock the doors right away. Redd came up to the driver side immediately going for the door handle.

"Open up this mothafuckin door!" he ordered. Fire seemed to dance in his eyes and his mouth was wet like a rabid animal.

Crying hysterically and shaking, Miki managed to ignite the car to life.

Redd beating on the car window with his gun, shook her up even more.

"Bitch, if you don't open up this goddamn door!"

Miki put the car in reverse and like a mad woman backed out of the driveway. Redd was still yelling and fuming. She quickly put the car in drive and took off.

Looking in the rearview mirror, she could see Redd run back into the house. *He's coming after me*, she thought.

Driving as cautious as possible without putting herself in danger, Miki sped through the neighborhood. Sure enough, Redd had jumped in his car and was closing the distance between them.

Miki ran through stop signs and traffic lights. She wasn't surprised to see that Redd didn't allow the rules of the road to stop him either. Hoping that she could lose him, she waited until the last minute to change lanes and enter the interstate heading North on I-65.

Redd was right behind her. She hoped the people witnessing this car chase would have enough sense to call into the authorities and report them. Where were the police that always hid out of view to trap people with speeding tickets?

Miki would be glad to pass by one of them at that moment.

Miki headed straight for her sister's house. Still weaving in and out of traffic, Miki somehow made it to her sister's house in one piece. Barely putting the car in park, Miki jumped out and ran for the front door. She began pounding on the door while ringing the doorbell simultaneously.

"Open up the door!" she cried out. She looked over her shoulders and saw Redd coming down the street. Frantically, she started banging on the door. "Hurry up! Please!"

Redd threw his car in park. As soon as he jumped out of his vehicle, he aimed his gun at Miki's back. In that very second, Gary was opening the door. Miki fell into the house just as a bullet made contact with the door's trim.

"What the fuck!" Gary exclaimed with alarm.

"Shut the door! It's Redd!" Miki cried hysterically. Without questioning Gary slammed the door shut.

Maddie asked, "What the hell is going on?"

"Call the police!" Miki demanded.

It was then Maddie observed her sister's condition. "Oh my God Miki! What happened to you?"

Gary got on the phone. When the dispatcher answered he said, "Uh yeah, we need a car out here as soon as possible...Uhm, yeah 545 Brookwood Drive...Yeah, there's a man outside my home who just fired a gun at my door..."

Téa came running toward the front, "Mommy!"

Miki was delighted to see her daughter. She went to Téa and embraced her tightly as tears streamed down her face.

Maddie explained, "I got her from Mama's since she

wanted to come—"

She was interrupted by the pounding on the door immediately followed by Redd's booming voice, "Miki! Bring your stupid ass out here, you dumb bitch!"

Maddie grabbed Téa up in her arms, "Come on baby. Let's see if we can make your mommy something to eat."

The pounding on the door never stopped; nor did the shouting. Miki shouted back, "Get away from the door! The police are coming. I'm done Redd."

"Come out this fuckin house!" he responded with one hard bang.

Miki broke down into heavy sobbing.

"Stop playing bitch! You gon make me fuck every mothafuckin body up in this goddamn house, you stupid hoe!"

Gary stepped up and said, "I think you should get away from my door and leave my property."

"Fuck you, you four-eyed bitch!" Redd barked.

Ten minutes later the police finally showed up. Redd's defiance and his delusional invincibility wouldn't let him leave like a sensible person would have. He didn't make his arrest easy.

After Redd was read his rights and was escorted to the back seat of the patrol car, officers came over to question Miki. Gary and Maddie were right there consoling her and encouraging her to do the right thing and tell the complete truth. Afterwards, Miki had to be taken to the hospital for examination and to receive medical attention for her injuries.

Bebe had shown up at the hospital ready to kill Redd. When he saw Miki, his heart dropped. Redd banged her up pretty bad. Her top lip had doubled in size and she had broken blood vessels in her left eye and she had a right ulnar fracture. Not to mention the several purple and red bruises that decorated her body and a concussion she suffered from Redd punching her in her head.

Redd was arrested and charged with possession of a firearm as a felon, interference with a 911 call, two counts of aggravated kidnapping with one being especially aggravated, and aggravated domestic assault. His bond was set at $120,000 and because it was domestic violence he was required to be held for twelve hours before he could be released. He had the money to bond out. Besides his uncle was a bondsman. And although the house was in Miki's name, staying there wasn't safe. She went back to the house and got as much as she could for her and Téa.

Later that night at Bebe's place, when the house was still, and everyone was asleep Miki eased into bed with Bebe.

"You okay?" Bebe asked.

She nodded. She laid directly under his arm resting her head on his chest. "Are you okay?"

"I'm good. I wanted to beat Redd's ass today but I'm over it now."

Miki chuckled. "I'm so glad it didn't get to that point because you would be in jail right now too."

"Well he's gone now," Bebe commented. He began rubbing her arm. He asked, "Are you going back this time?"

"Nah...I don't think so."

"Good," he said. "There's something I've been wanting to talk to you about."

"What is that?"

"Marriage."

Chapter 22

Life sure did have a way with working itself out. Miki was happy, finally for the first time. At twenty-seven weeks pregnant, Miki had a glow that brightened any room she walked into. She was in love and ready to make things official with her true love, Blyss "Bebe" Blakemore. They recently discovered that they were having a baby boy. The first time she went for an ultrasound the baby was stubborn and didn't want to reveal his sex. Shortly after, Miki was diagnosed with gestational diabetes; therefore, routine ultrasounds were necessary. It was on one of her ultrasound visits that they learned they were having a boy.

It was May, the Saturday before Memorial Day. Bebe's house was noisy with laughter and chatter as the women busied themselves preparing for this wedding.

Ava was already in tears. "You look so pretty Miki."

"Mama, will you get away from me," Miki said playfully swatting at Ava. She was getting her hair and makeup done by Kat.

Kat said, "She's gon be the most beautiful pregnant bride you've ever seen."

"Really Kat? You had to slide the pregnant part in there," Miki asked wryly.

"Well you are," Kat said. Although she was now living in Atlanta, Kat couldn't miss this special occasion for nothing. She was honored to be a part of the bridal party and the head hairdresser.

"Where are my shoes!" Kizzie hollered.

"All of the shoes are over there by the fireplace. Your name should be on them," Maddie answered.

Joyce stood there watching Kat work her magic on Miki. "She is pretty. Just a'glowing."

Miki smiled. Kennedi came into the living room where the women had transformed it into a beauty salon/dressing room. Kennedi's Shirley Temple curls bounced as she walked. She wore a frown.

Deja asked, "What's wrong with you Kennedi?"

"Where's Téa? Téa not coming?" Kennedi asked.

"She's on her way," Miki said. "Her other granny got her. Somebody give me my phone because she should have been here."

As Deja passed Miki her phone, it rung. Miki looked down at it and smiled. She answered, "What worrisome ass boy?"

"I know you ain't calling me worrisome and I ain't no boy," Bebe said.

"You done called me like fifty times."

"No, I haven't. Maybe forty-nine, but not fifty."

Miki laughed. "What do you want?"

"I just wanted to hear your voice and talk to Mikina Monroe for the last time," he said softly.

"Ahh! You do?"

"I love you, Miki."

"I love you too."

"You know I'm not even nervous. Are you?" he asked.

"I got jitters from excitement," she said.

"You're nervous," Bebe said.

Miki could hear the rowdiness of the men in the background. "What y'all doing over there? Y'all sound like y'all still at the club."

"You know how these niggas are," he said. He asked, "So are you good?"

"I'm fine."

"How's my son?"

"He's fine. He ain't moving now but I bet during the ceremony he's gonna be all over the place. You know how he is."

"He gets active at the wrong damn times. Is Téa there yet?"

"Not yet. I was just about to call Mona when you called."

"Why they tripping? Do I need to drive over there and get her?"

"No Bebe. You're the last person that need to go over there. I got it. She'll be here," Miki said.

"Well go ahead and take care of that."

"Okay Elmo," Miki teased.

Bebe laughed, "Don't be calling me that shit."

"Tickle me Elmo."

"Bye man. I love you."

"Bye. Love you too," Miki laughed as she ended the call. She immediately dialed Mona's number.

"Hello?"

"Hey Mona. I was just calling—"

Mona cut her off. "She's on her way."

"Okay," Miki said a bit insulted by Mona's rudeness. The call was ended.

"What?" Ava asked.

"She talking snappy," Miki said.

"She still bitter?" Maddie asked.

"She's always been bitter, but I thought she put it aside for the sake of Téa," Miki said. "She's the only reason I even let Téa go over there. Everybody else can kiss my ass."

Miki's phone rang again. This time it was from an unknown number. Miki answered cautiously, "Hello?"

"Don't hang up," Redd said. "I just wanna talk to you."

Miki didn't say anything because she didn't want to alarm everybody around her. Redd wasn't supposed to be nowhere around her or even calling her. For three months he had been obeying the rules of the order of protection. Miki hadn't heard a peep out of him. They were still in the process of going to court for his charges, but he hired a good lawyer and had been pushing the court dates off prolonging Redd's freedom.

Redd said, "I know what today is and I just wanted to congratulate you. I ain't tryna come at you in the wrong way or nothing. I've been away from you like I'm supposed to be. I got Téa and I'm bringing her to you. When I pull up can you come out and get her. I don't want your family tripping and shit tryna call the police."

"Okay."

"I'll call you when I'm there," he said.

"Okay," was all she could say. The call ended.

"Who was that?" Maddie asked.

"Mona calling me back," Miki lied.

Minutes later Redd texted her: I'm outside.

Miki got up and said, "I'm getting Téa." The ladies continued to get dressed and made up.

Miki went outside, and spotted Redd's SUV pulled up along the yard of the neighbor's house. She went to the passenger side door. She heard the door unlock. He let the window down a little to say, "Get in real quick."

Against her better judgment she did. She thought, what could it hurt. Redd seemed to have gotten the picture and had moved on.

"Hey," she said.

"Hey Mommy," Téa said from the backseat.

"Hey. You need to get in the house and get prettied up."

"Wait," Redd said. He looked intensely into Miki's eyes. "I just want to apologize to you for everything I done in the past."

Miki gave him a nod of acknowledgment. She was hearing his words.

"You know I sit and I think about how things coulda been different."

Miki said, "I used to tell you that all the time Redd."

"Miki, you knew I had issues. All I wanted was for you to be there for me and love me. Instead you was busy loving and fucking on another nigga."

"I was there for you. I took your abuse for years. Way

before I met Bebe."

"You wasn't thinking about leaving me until that nigga came into the picture."

"Redd, you were mistreating me. I shoulda left sooner than what I did. I need to go because we shouldn't even be talking to one another."

Redd locked the doors. Miki began to panic. Was this nigga going to kidnap her on her wedding day? "What are you doing?"

Redd's expression changed to one mixed with despair, anger and hurt. "I can't let you marry him."

"Stop Redd!" Miki hollered and unlocked the door. He locked it back before she could reach for the handle.

He said, "Téa is still in the car. You get out, I pull off with her."

"I'll call the police," Miki threatened. "I tried to trust you, Redd. I coulda called the police when you first called. But I tried to give you the benefit of the doubt."

"You were always stupid and fell for my shit," he sneered.

Miki grew angry; more so with herself than with him. "Redd don't do this. Please."

"That nigga ain't' getting you or my daughter. Fuck that. And how you know that's not my baby you're carrying?"

"Cause it's not," she snapped. "C'mon Téa."

Next thing Miki knew there was a gun in Redd's hand and he was waving it as he spoke, "You know...I figure by the time this court shit over with I'ma be doing a lot of time. I ain't tryna go back to prison, Miki. And I've told your bitch ass that over and mothafuckin over. I wasn't going back. And I meant it. And I meant what I said by I ain't letting him have you and Téa. I'll kill us all before I do that."

Miki was frozen with fear. Why did she come out to the car? Why had she been so foolish?

"Where your man at now?" Redd asked pointing the gun in her face and pulling the hammer back.

"Redd," she said nervously. She began to shake as she prayed to herself hoping someone would notice she had been gone too long.

"Don't call my name now. You did this. You!"

"I didn't do nothing!"

"Who the fuck you yelling at?"

She leaned against the door to be as far away from him as possible. She looked back at Téa who was trying not to make a noise but was crying. "You scaring Téa."

Redd started speaking real low, whispering under his breath. Miki couldn't' make out what he was saying.

"Redd?"

If Miki could tell anyone, what Redd did next was the most horrific thing she could ever witness. She felt helpless and in that moment, she wanted to die when he turned the gun on Téa and shot her. Miki witnessed the life leave her daughter's body instantly.

Redd turned to a screaming Miki and shot her twice; one in the chest and one in the stomach. He then took his own life.

"What's that?" Maddie asked fearfully. "That was close. Where's Miki?"

They all looked at one another then bolted for the front door. When they got in the yard they didn't see any signs of Miki. Kizzie said, "Ain't that Redd's truck?"

"Oh my God!" Ava screamed. "Go see if Miki is in there."

Maddie and Kizzie both ran over to the SUV and started beating on the tinted windows and tried to open the door. "Miki!"

Maddie went around to the driver's side to try the doors. Kizzie and Kat both let out a blood-curdling scream as the passenger door opened and Miki fell out with two open wounds spurting out blood. Before she hit the ground, Kat caught her. Miki was trying to say something, but her lungs were filling quickly with her own blood. Nothing but gurgles came out. She managed to say in her last breath, "Bebe..."

Kat couldn't believe this day had come. It was like a bad dream had become reality. Just when the clouds had rolled back, and the sun was smiling down on her best friend, the storm returned. In the worst way.

If Kat had known that Miki was going to meet Redd, her daughter's father that afternoon, Kat would have accompanied Miki. But Miki didn't alert anybody that she felt worried. Knowing Miki, she wanted to keep the peace. She wouldn't want the day disrupted by Redd's antics. She especially didn't want to upset her husband to be, Blyss "Bebe" Blakemore.

It was stupid Miki, Kat thought as she blinked out tears. They blurred her vision but the two coffins, the larger one holding Miki while the smaller one contained her five-year-old daughter Téa, stuck out boldly forever embedding an image in Kat's mind: they were gone. Greater Victory Baptist Church was filled with family and friends mourning the loss of two beautiful beings. Their deaths came as a shock to many. Miki had moved on. She no longer lived under Redd's hold, a hold that had choked the life out of Miki for years. Miki suffered physical, mental, verbal, and emotional abuse from Redd ever since she was eighteen. She had finally met a man that gave her enough courage to walk away from Redd.

There was no questioning that the love between Miki and Bebe was real. It had been a quick connect but Bebe didn't want to waste any time. The two started a love affair that grew into an undeniable unbreakable love for one another. That was why after nine months of meeting the two were making it official. Bebe was making Miki, Mrs. Blyss Blakemore.

Redd was still harboring evilness, hatred, jealousy, hurt, and pain. He wasn't allowing Miki to escape his grasp that easy. And he definitely wasn't letting Bebe just walk away with his woman despite the fact Miki had walked away from him four months ago.

Everyone speculated that when Miki called Mona, Redd's mother about getting Téa over to the house so she could get ready for the wedding that was taking place that day, that Redd had already devised his plan. Miki had been at her new home she shared with Bebe getting ready with the other ladies in the bridal party. Bebe had been at Maddie's house with all of the men. Instead of Mona bringing Téa to Miki, Redd had been the one to bring Téa. He asked Miki if she could come out to the car to get Téa.

Miki was still dressed in a white t-shirt and cargo capris. The roller-set curls in her hair were still intact. She wore pink flip flops on her freshly manicured feet. She was glowing and genuinely happy. Redd's presence didn't even bother her like he had in the past. When Miki didn't return right away, Kat thought it was odd but didn't think to act on it. Minutes later the gunshots rang out: POW! POW! POW! ...POW!

The first shot ended Téa's life instantly as it tore through her small torso. Miki's scream had been horrific and bone-chilling. So shocked and confused, she wasn't thinking about her life being in danger too. The second shot went straight into her stomach ending the life that was thriving there. Redd put the third round in her heart. Redd screamed something inaudible before taking his own life.

Kat along with everyone else was concerned about Bebe. The whole thing had hit him the hardest. Kat had never seen a grown man break down the way he did. Bebe, who was always so vocal and tough and quick-tempered had been reduced to helplessness and in a pitiful emotional state. He wasn't talking, eating, or leaving out of his bedroom. He laid in bed every day all day not responding to anybody. He clutched a photo of Téa with Kennedi, his daughter and Téa's best friend and he held onto a picture of Miki and him. In the photo Bebe hugged Miki from behind, his hands palming her protruding belly. Miki had been seven months pregnant with Bebe's child when Redd killed her. Redd knew exactly what he was doing when he made sure her womb was penetrated with a bullet.

Everyone said Bebe would probably never be the same. It was the saddest thing. A man who was once full of life with enough fight in him to take on an army was stricken with grief and despair. He felt defeated. Lately living didn't interest Bebe. Not even for his two kids, BJ and Kennedi.

Bebe hadn't attended visitation and no one was sure if he would actually attend the memorial service and burial. He and both his children were absent the first hour of service. Pastor

Marc Thomas was in the middle of a soul touching spirit moving sermon when Bebe finally showed up. He nor BJ and Kennedi were appropriately dressed for a funeral. All three were in very casual, very ruffled lounging attire like they had just got out of bed. Kennedi wore the saddest, longest face for her usually bright heart-shaped face. Her black hair was disheveled about her head in a messy ponytail. She held Téa's favorite Dora doll and Téa's favorite sequined *Hello Kitty* purse.

The church eased into a quietness as everyone watched the trio make their way towards the altar where the two caskets sat. Even Pastor Thomas let his voice trail off. The choir and organist filled the emptiness with very soft singing and a tune.

Bebe picked Kennedi up into his arms. They went to Téa first. Kennedi placed the doll and purse inside the coffin with the sleeping Téa. She cried to her daddy, "When her wake up her can have Dora since my can't be there."

Anybody that was close enough to hear was overwhelmed with emotions and unable to hold back. Kat cried even harder when Bebe went to Miki and placed the three-carat diamond bridal set his best man Dinky was holding for him just six days before on Miki's chest. The ring that would have been placed on Miki's left ring finger sealing the deal, making his and Miki's love official.

It was clear Bebe had been crying already. His mother, Joyce was already on alert and was moving when Bebe noticed the small decorative ceramic box placed just so in the coffin with Miki. Bebe's cousins, Abe and Dinky, were right there to assist Joyce when Bebe lost it. In the box were the cremated remains of his child that he would never get to meet or raise. There had been question about the paternity of the baby boy

Miki was carrying. It wasn't a one hundred percent firm belief that Bebe was indeed the father. There was a slight possibility that Redd could have been the father, but Bebe didn't care one way or the other. Even if it had been Redd's child, Bebe was going to give the child his name. But because the baby died, Bebe would never know for sure if the baby was his true offspring.

Bebe was so angry with Miki. He didn't think if he could ever forgive her for doing something so stupid. Why? He asked over and over in his head. She was so gullible, so naïve and just wanted to believe the best in people.

This was the most hurt and grief Bebe had ever felt. He didn't even feel this way when his father died. Miki had been the one. He had been in love and it felt good. He was hurt and heartbroken. He didn't think it was even possible to love again. Just like that, she was gone. Her, Téa and his son.

Praise be to the God and Father of our Lord Jesus Christ, the Father of compassion and the God of all comfort, who comforts us in all our troubles, so that we can comfort those in any trouble with the comfort we ourselves have received from God. For just as the sufferings of Christ flow over into our lives, so also through Christ our comfort overflows

--2 Corinthians 1:3-5

CPSIA information can be obtained
at www.ICGtesting.com
Printed in the USA
LVHW01s2043110718
583386LV00015B/989/P